TUBBY
THE FAT CLOWN

STEPHEN GNOZA
ANDREW VITA

120
pages

Printed in the United States of America

Second Edition.
First Printing, 2017

ISBN 978-1-947197-00-8

120pages
Subway Sites LLC
PO BOX 231548
New York, NY 10023

www.120pages.com

HOW TO READ A SCREENPLAY

A screenplay is written to show, not tell. Screenplays convey how a film will play out. The story unfolds through the dialogue and actions of the characters. As such, words are used economically. There is less description than you would find in a novel, as those details are typically handled during the production process. There is very little exposition; the screenplay doesn't provide any information that an audience watching the film wouldn't receive.

Therefore, as you read, visualize a film in your mind and "see" it as if you were watching a film.

If you're not familiar with the screenplay format, here are some things to know:

SCENE HEADINGS

Scene headings describe where the action takes place, the time of day, and sometimes additional details, such as if the action takes place in a flashback or as part of a montage.

For example:

```
INT. SAMMY'S HOUSE - DAY
```

"INT" indicates the action is indoors. "SAMMY'S HOUSE" tells us the action is in a woman's house. "DAY" tells us that it is daytime.

```
EXT. PARK - NIGHT
```

"EXT" indicates the action is outdoors. "PARK" tells us we are in a park. "NIGHT" tells us that it is the evening.

Other time descriptions may be used, such as "SAME" to indicate action taking place simultaneously or "LATER" to indicate action taking place moments later, after a brief jump in time.

CAPITALIZED WORDS

Throughout a screenplay, you may come across CAPITALIZED WORDS. These generally indicate the introduction of a new character, that the camera should pay attention to a particular item/sound/person/location, or that we are moving into a specific place within the location.

For example:

```
John turns.  He sees SALLY, the most beautiful girl he has ever
laid eyes on.  In her hands, she holds AN ADORABLE PUPPY.
```

DIALOGUE

Dialogue is written by centering a character's name with their spoken words appearing beneath their name. For example:

```
                    JOHN
          You found Charlie!
```

PARANTHETICALS

Between the character's name and dialogue, you may see text in parenthesis. This indicates some specific direction about how the dialogue is to be read or some specific action that takes place during the delivery of the dialogue.

```
                    JOHN
              (eyes watering)
          You found Charlie!
```

OTHER TERMS

Here are some other terms you may come across when reading a screenplay:

`(O.S.)` or `(O.C.)` – Off-screen or off-camera indicates that we do not see a character when dialogue is heard

`(V.O.)` – Indicates voiceover. This is dialogue we hear, but the speaker is not physically present in the same location as the action

`(CONT'D)` – Indicates that the same character is continuing to deliver a line of dialogue after an action, scene change, or page break

`(MORE)` – Indicates that the dialogue from the character continues on the next page

`POV` – Indicates that we see the action through a defined point of view

`SUPERIMPOSE` – Indicates that we see text on screen, often to define a time or location

`MONTAGE` – Indicates rapid cutting of different scenes in a sequence, such as any training sequence in a Rocky movie

`(beat)` – Indicates that a character takes a brief pause before continuing dialogue

                                                    FADE IN:

EXT. KIMMY'S HOUSE, BACKYARD - DAY

A little girl's birthday party. Children and adults are
gathered around a patio table. A vanilla cake topped with
strawberries sits before KIMMY, a 9-year-old girl.

The crowd finishes singing a birthday song and claps.

Kimmy's mother, VANESSA -- 40's and pretty -- leans over her
shoulder.

                    VANESSA
          Happy Birthday, sweetheart. Make a
          wish.

Kimmy ponders her wish. She surveys the crowd surrounding
her, almost looking beyond them, as if anticipating
something...

Kimmy takes a deep breath. She is about to blow out the
candles...

BUT THE CAKE IS SNATCHED FROM RIGHT IN FRONT OF HER!

CHAOS follows! Adults scramble. There is SHOUTING. A
table is knocked over.

Several children are laughing. Others are crying.

Kimmy's dad, BRYAN -- 40's, slightly overweight, and a
little intoxicated -- bolts for the front of the house, beer
can in hand.

EXT. SUBURBAN STREETS - DAY

Bryan races down the street. Several other adults follow.

                    BRYAN
          Get back here, you fat thief!

In a futile attempt, Bryan pitches the beer can forward.

Ahead of him, TUBBY -- 30's, over 400 pounds and dressed as
a clown -- runs away.

Tubby HONKS his big, red nose.

A TAXI CAB SKIDS AROUND THE CORNER.

With great difficulty, Tubby attempts to wedge himself into
the backseat of the cab.

                                                  (CONTINUED)

2.

THE MOB OF PARENTS DRAWS NEARER.

The taxi driver, RAOUL, climbs out of the front seat and
pushes the fat clown into the backseat.

INT. TAXI CAB - DAY

Tubby adjust himself as Raoul enters the driver's seat. The
car JOLTS forward.

Tubby looks out the back window: the mob of angry parents
gets smaller and smaller.

                    RAOUL
          Tubby, my friend, have you put on
          weight?

Tubby shoves a piece of the stolen birthday cake into his
mouth before answering.

                    TUBBY
          Now, that's a rude question!
               (beat)
          What makes you say that?

                    RAOUL
          No reason.

EXT. SUBURBAN STREETS - DAY

The cab's back bumper drags along the pavement, creating
awful SCRAPING NOISES and SPARKS.

EXT. KIMMY'S HOUSE, BACKYARD - DAY

The yard is now a mess. Kimmy and her friends are all
smiles.

JACOB -- a 9-year-old boy -- high-fives Kimmy.

                    JACOB
          Kimmy, that was awesome!

The other children voice their agreement. Kimmy blushes.
This has been the best birthday ever.

Bryan and the other parents re-enter the yard, exhausted and
disappointed.

                    BRYAN
          I swear to God --

He kicks a lawn chair over.

Vanessa puts her arms around her husband.

                    VANESSA
          Don't be so mad. Kimmy and her
          friends thought it was hilarious.

Bryan SLAMS a fist on a patio table. This silences
everyone. Tension is in the air.

                    BRYAN
          I will not tolerate this kind of
          behavior in my own house! When I
          am sworn in as mayor of this town,
          I will not tolerate it anywhere!

Vanessa rolls her eyes and walks off. As she does:

                    VANESSA
          Give it a rest, Bryan.

Bryan reaches into a cooler, pulls a can of beer, and pops
it open.

                    BRYAN
              (addressing parents)
          When I'm mayor, I'll protect you
          all from crime like this. It'll be
          like the whole town is my home. I
          can come into any one of your
          houses, raid your fridge... I'm
          gonna make it a law you have to all
          give me your wifi passwords --

                    VANESSA
              (from inside house)
          I think what you mean is you're
          going to lock up those gangsters.

                    BRYAN
          Right. Yes. We'll get that fat
          clown off the street.

                    VANESSA
              (from inside house)
          Organized crime, honey. Not clown
          crime.

The beer can crumples in his hands.

                    BRYAN
          Crime is crime! It's all the same!

Vanessa emerges from the house with a second cake.

4.

                    VANESSA
          Here's the backup cake!

The tension breaks. The children yell, applaud, and rush to
the cake.

Bryan finds himself left standing next to another father.

                    BRYAN
          I hear your house has a really big
          screen TV.

                    OTHER FATHER
          Look! Strawberry filling!

The other father rushes away from Bryan and toward the cake.

EXT. EDGE OF CIRCUS GROUNDS - DAY

The cab pulls up to the camp grounds, noisily dragging the
back bumper on the ground.

Tubby struggles out of the backseat. The backend of the car
immediately lifts up off the ground.

Raoul rolls down the window and leans out.

                    RAOUL
          Tubby, when are you going to move
          on from this dump?

Tubby gazes at the circus: a VILLAGE OF BROKEN-DOWN
TRAILERS AND RUNDOWN TENTS. It is LITTERED WITH TRASH.

                    TUBBY
          I see potential.

                    RAOUL
          I left the circus nine years ago.
          I've made more money driving my cab
          than I ever made driving the clown
          car.

                    TUBBY
          Just use your imagination! It's a
          fixer-upper.

                    RAOUL
          C'mon, man. What's keeping you
          here?

EXT. CIRCUS GROUNDS - DAY

Outside of a beaten down trailer, a large woman sits in a
rocking chair. She drinks sweet tea and stares up at the
sky. This is PUDGEY -- 30's, overweight, a female Tubby.

                    PUDGEY
               (singing)
          There is beauty deep below, just
          like a fried oreo...

                    TUBBY (O.C.)
          Music to my stomach!

Pudgey is startled. Then, she sees Tubby approaching and is
slightly embarrassed.

                    TUBBY
          What are you doing out here?

                    PUDGEY
          Alazander suggested that I think of
          a new way to contribute to the
          show. You know, now that my
          unicycle is broken.

Tubby rolls his eyes at the sound of Alazander's name.

                    TUBBY
          Alazander? Who cares what that
          magician says? Why doesn't he
          just pull a unicycle out of a hat?

                    PUDGEY
          Jealous?

                    TUBBY
          Can you really trust someone who
          makes poor little doves disappear?
          Besides, Ringmaster Pepper will buy
          you a new unicycle when he can.

                    PUDGEY
          Pepper says times are tough and we
          need to tighten our belts.

Tubby pats his large belly.

                    TUBBY
          I don't think that's possible!

6.

                    PUDGEY
          Well, in the meantime, I thought
          maybe I'd sing.

Pudgey smiles at Tubby.

                    PUDGEY
          Ya still got cake on your face, do
          you know that?

Tubby rubs his hand over his face, finds the bit of cake,
and then eats it.

                    TUBBY
     Mmmm.

                    PUDGEY
          Some day, you're going to steal
          cake from the wrong person.

                    TUBBY
          You're just jealous I didn't bring
          you any.

                    PUDGEY
          That would have been romantic.

                    TUBBY
               (suggestively)
          It had strawberries and whipped
          cream.

Tubby belches.

                    PUDGEY
          You're disgusting.

                    TUBBY
          I could use a little more desert.
          Why don't you pour some sugar on
          me?

                    PUDGEY
          I'll be right back.

Pudgey stands up and enters her trailer, leaving the door
open behind her.

                    TUBBY
               (to himself)
          It must be my lucky day!

Pudgey emerges and hands him a five pound bag of sugar.

                    TUBBY
          What am I supposed to do with this?

                    PUDGEY
          Wait a sec.

Pudgey disappears inside, then emerges with a large spoon.

                    PUDGEY
          Here.

                    TUBBY
          You know the way to a fat clown's
          heart.

Tubby opens the bag and begins eating the sugar by the
spoonful.

                    PUDGEY
          Okay, sugar. Go home and get some
          rest. We have a big show tomorrow.

INT. CIRCUS TENT - DAY

A single spotlight focuses on a platform in the center of
the tent. PEPPER -- late 60's, short, tired -- stands on a
platform. He is dressed in a ringmaster costume, colorful
and complete with a top hat.

                    PEPPER
          Ladies and gentlemen, welcome to
          Pepper's Super Groove-tastic
          Circus! I am Pepper, the
          ringmaster and your host! We have
          an amazing show for you today!
          Without further ado, prepare to be
          astonished!

A montage of the circus show follows, including:

Tubby running around an obstacle course, falling over
himself...

Pudgey, in a penguin costume, stands off to the side,
clapping and waddling. She doesn't do much at all...

Tubby trying to squeeze into the clown car, an old
Volkswagen Beetle...

Tight-rope walkers juggling lit torches...

ALAZANDER -- 30's, slender and pale -- waves his magician's
wand, making a dove disappear into a fireball...

8.

BILLY the animal-tamer lets the tiger loose and uses a whip
and chair to control him...

THE AMAZING FLYING ROBERT gets shot out of a cannon...

Big band music accompanies the entire show...

The show concludes with a big music hit and Pepper is back,
center-stage.

                    PEPPER
          Thank you all for coming! Good
          night!

For the first time, we see the audience: A HANDFUL OF
CHINESE TOURISTS.

                    CHINESE TOURIST #1
          What he say?

                    CHINESE TOURIST #2
          Eat tiger?

Chinese Tourist #1 points at Tubby.

                    CHINESE TOURIST #1
          That one. He eat enough.

Tubby is not amused.

INT. CIRCUS TENT, BACKSTAGE - DAY

Tubby, Pudgey, Alazander, and the other performers enter a
backstage area.

                    TUBBY
          That guy has point about eating the
          tiger.

Billy cracks his whip.

                    BILLY
          You are not eating Lilly!

                    TUBBY
          Fine. Don't have a cow!
               (beat)
          Oh, great. Now, I'm thinking about
          a cheeseburger deluxe from Steve's
          BBQ.

                         BILLY
          That's all you ever think about.

Tubby reclines onto a beanbag chair.

                         TUBBY
          I thought the show went well.

                         ALAZANDER
                    (sarcastically)
          It's a good thing Pepper was able
          to sell a whole three tickets.

                         TUBBY
          Hey, Alazander, I don't see you
          conjuring up any dollar bills.

                         PUDGEY
          Come on, boys, don't get started.

Tubby surveys the room and notices all the glum faces.

                         TUBBY
          What's the matter with everyone? We
          just put on a great show!

                         BILLY
          Pepper's gotta sell a whole lot
          more tickets or we're done for.

Billy lets his whip fall to the ground.

                         TUBBY
          Don't let your whip go limp. Be
          optimistic!

                         ALAZANDER
          Pepper should overhaul the
          show, bring in some new acts, maybe
          some new talent.

                         TUBBY
          We already have great talent.

                         ALAZANDER
          No one wants to pay good money
          to see a fatso.

Tubby looks genuinely hurt.

                         TUBBY
          What does my weight have to do
          with --

10.

Pudgey quickly steps forward.

                    PUDGEY
          Alazander's point is that the show
          needs to evolve with the times.

                    TUBBY
          You're on the warlock's side now?

                    PUDGEY
          Children don't need a circus for
          entertainment. Not as it exists
          right now. It needs to
          offer something they can't get
          online!

                    TUBBY
          Tiger meat?

                    BILLY
          You are not to eat my tiger, you
          bloated buffoon!

                    ROBERT
          You can probably order tiger meat
          off the internet.

                    ALAZANDER
          I was thinking more along the lines
          of burlesque dancing.

Pudgey glares at him disapprovingly.

                    ROBERT
          Sweet! A stripper!

                    BILLY
          Okay, but my whip is for tigers
          only.

Pudgey rolls her eyes and turns from the crowd.

                    PUDGEY
          I've had enough of this
          conversation.

Pudgey exits.

                    ALAZANDER
          Well, well. _Now_ there's no reason
          to keep hanging around here.

There is a BURST OF SMOKE AND LIGHT, and Alazader has
disappeared.

                    TUBBY
          Can't he walk away like a <u>normal</u>
          person?

INT. PEPPER'S TRAILER - DAY

Pepper is making some tea. There is a KNOCK on the door.

                    PEPPER
          Yes?

The door opens.

                    TUBBY
          Pepper, may I come in?

                    PEPPER
          You can try.

Pepper watches with disgust as Tubby struggles to maneuver
himself through the doorway. He is too wide to easily pass
through. The trailer SHAKES VIOLENTLY.

Pepper moans and turns back to his tea.

Finally, Tubby makes his way in, with a stumble. He catches
his breath.

                    PEPPER
          Well, Tubby, what is it?

                    TUBBY
          Is the circus in danger of closing?
          Are we going to be out of jobs?

                    PEPPER
          Ha! Finally focusing your eyes on
          something other than childrens'
          birthday cakes!

Tubby is genuinely confused.

                    PEPPER
          Yes! The circus is in deep shit.
          We can't sell tickets! The place
          is falling apart. I've got no
          money left to invest.

As Pepper speaks, Tubby eyes a tiny slice of CHEESECAKE on
the kitchen counter.

                        PEPPER (CONT'D)
              Insurance costs keep skyrocketing.
              I have to pay "protection" payments
              to that gangster, Big Lou.

Tubby eyes are now fixated on the cheesecake.

                        PEPPER (CONT'D)
              Tubby, there comes a time in a
              man's life when he looks back and
              considers the ledger of his
              accomplishments and shortcomings.

Pepper sits down with his tea, and stares off in the
distance, almost speaking to himself.

Tubby, preoccupied with the cheesecake, doesn't hear what
Pepper is saying.

                        PEPPER (CONT'D)
              Hopefully, at the end, the sum is
              in his favor. And he has
              contributed something to the world.

Tubby is sweating over the prospect of cheesecake.

                        PEPPER (CONT'D)
              Or has a legacy. I like to think
              the measure of a man is having
              something to pass on and someone to
              pass it on to.

Tubby is starting to fidget, barely able to control himself.

                        PEPPER (CONT'D)
              I never found love in life. Sure,
              there were a few one-night stands
              here and there. But no
              children. Not that I know of,
              anyway. No one who will take over
              the circus.

Pepper laughs to himself. Tubby is tormented.

                        PEPPER (CONT'D)
              I suppose it would be cruel to dump
              the circus on a child. It's a
              liability. A drain on life and
              dreams. It's like a student loan,
              but with a bunch of weirdos you
              can't get out of your life.

Pepper takes a careful, meditative sip of tea.

Tubby's giant red shoes shake.

                    PEPPER (CONT'D)
          I've come to terms with the fact
          that I will die a lonely, old,
          indebted failure.

Tubby can no longer resist! He darts across the trailer -
causing it to shake - and devours the piece of cheesecake.

Pepper leaps up from his seat.

                    PEPPER
          What is wrong with you?!

Tubby turns innocently to him, cheesecake on his fat face
with an expression that says, "Me?"

A BURST OF SMOKE AND LIGHT! Alazander has appeared.

                    ALAZANDER
          Ringmaster, there is still hope for
          the circus.

Alazander gestures toward Tubby, who is licking cheesecake
off of his face.

                    ALAZANDER (CONT'D)
          Do you really want your legacy to
          be in the hands of idiots like him?

                    TUBBY
          I'm not an idiot. I graduated at
          the top of my class from clown
          college.

Alazander produces a box from within his robes.

                    ALAZANDER
          Here.

Tubby takes the box and opens it. His face lights up!

                    TUBBY
          Macaroons!

                    ALAZANDER
          It is time to bring the circus into
          modern times. Cut the clowns. Add
          more acrobatics, laser-lights,
          special effects to dazzle the minds
          of children. And burlesque.

14.

Tubby is horrified.

                    TUBBY
          (with stuffed mouth)
     You're not seriously considering
     this, are you?

Pepper doesn't answer. He gazes into his teacup.

                    TUBBY
     Pepper, a circus is made up
     of clowns, and lion-tamers and
     people being shot out of cannons
     and --

Alazander produces a brown paper bag and hands it to Tubby.

                    ALAZANDER
     Here.

Tubby looks inside the bag.

                    TUBBY
     Chocolate chip muffin!

                    ALAZANDER
     Ringmaster, we must try. The
     circus won't survive another few
     months.

                    PEPPER
     It's a decent thought.

                    TUBBY
     No, it's not! It's as indecent as
     a peanut butter, ham, and kale
     sandwich!

                    PEPPER
     Tubby, what we are doing is not
     working.

                    TUBBY
     So you're going to let this
     charlatan wave his wand and change
     everything?

                    PEPPER
     I'm not saying it's the best thing
     to do, but we must consider all
     options --

Tubby throws down the empty brown paper bag.

                         TUBBY
          I'm not going to stay and listen to
          this!

Tubby goes to storm out of the trailer, but has a difficult
time squeezing through the doorway. Pepper and Alazander
watch in silence for a few awkward moments as Tubby
struggles. The entire trailer SHAKES.

INT. CUPCAKE HOUSE - NIGHT

Tubby is seated at a counter in a bakery/cafe. The
proprietor and head baker, MISS ROLLY -- 50's, plump,
motherly -- wanders over, carrying a rolling pin.

                         MISS ROLLY
          Rough day, Dumpling?

                         TUBBY
          Line 'em up.

Miss Rolly lines up a dozen cupcakes in front of Tubby, as
if they were shots. Tubby eats three of them in a few
seconds.

                         MISS ROLLY
          What's got you down?

Miss Rolly uses her rolling pin on some dough.

                         TUBBY
          The circus. Things are just not
          going the way I had hoped.

                         MISS ROLLY
          Things rarely are what we expect
          them to be.

She holds up a sheet of uncooked dough.

                         MISS ROLLY
          See, no one expects this to taste
          good. But by adding a little love
          and the right ingredients, it
          becomes mmm-mmm tasty.

Tubby eats a few more cupcakes.

                         MISS ROLLY
          If you don't like the way things
          are, change them. Most
          importantly...

The oven DINGS!

16.

                         MISS ROLLY
            ... strike while the oven is hot!

Tubby considers this and eats the remaining cupcakes.

Miss Rolly picks up some raw dough.

                         MISS ROLLY
            Life is like this dough. Flat,
            boring. It gets beaten with a
            rolling pin.

She proceeds to roughly manhandle the dough with the rolling
pin.

                         MISS ROLLY
            But when all is said and done, it
            rises into something beautiful and
            delicious.

She holds up a lovely loaf of bread. Tubby snatches the
loaf and takes a bite off the end.

                         TUBBY
            Life's delicious.

                         MISS ROLLY
            That's the spirit!

                         TUBBY
            And life is better with butter and
            lard!

Miss Rolly considers this, but is at a loss for words.

Tubby takes another big bite out of the bread.

EXT. TOWN SQUARE - DAY

A speaking platform has been erected in front of city hall.
The stage is decorated with bunting and other patriotic
details. A number of local politicians loiter on stage.

BEHIND STAGE, Bryan finishes reading a stack of index cards.
He hands the cards out toward his CAMPAIGN MANAGER.

                         BRYAN
            It sounds like a robot wrote this.

                         CAMPAIGN MANAGER
            It tested well. Just go with it.

She pushes the cards back to him. He rolls his eyes.

ON STAGE, Bryan appears to the sounds of applause. He
approaches a podium. Behind him, Vanessa, Kimmy, and
several politicians are seated.

                    BRYAN
          Today, I take over as mayor for a
          man who betrayed your trust,
          made deals with the gangsters that
          undermined our local businesses,
          and put our families in jeopardy.
          This special election puts a great
          challenge before me. Crime has
          been on the rise in our town, and
          has even penetrated our government.
          We're going to put an end to it.
          We will rid this town of <u>all</u> crime.
          In fact, I announce today, a one
          million dollar reward to anyone who
          can help us arrest the mob leader,
          Big Lou.

The crowd erupts into applause. Bryan motions to a man on
stage, SHERIFF BOB.

                    BRYAN
          If you have any information, please
          contact Sheriff Bob. Thank you.

Sheriff Bob gives a little wave.

Bryan steps away from the podium, ripping up the index cards
as he goes.

Then he stops. He returns to the podium.

                    BRYAN
          Oh, and just one more thing. We are
          going to get rid of <u>all crime</u>. And
          crime has many faces. Gangsters are
          obvious, but some faces are covered
          in makeup. And big red noses. And
          wear colorful wigs. There is
          nothing more un-American than
          birthday cakes being stolen!

The crowd is hesitant to applaud. A child cries.

                    BRYAN
          Okay. Thank you.

Bryan turns and hurriedly steps off stage.

18.

In the crowd, several local reporters, including a woman
named YOLANDA SCARLET, waves frantically to try to get
Bryan's attention. She pushes her way through the crowd.

                    SCARLET
          Excuse me, excuse me!

She gets near the stage and extends her audio recorder.

                    SCARLET
          Mr. Mayor! Yolanda Scarlet,
          evening news! Are you saying the
          circus folk are as dangerous as
          gangsters?

An official blocks her way to the stage as Bryan exits down
the back.

On stage, another official takes the mic.

                    OFFICIAL
          There will be no questions today.
          Thank you.

Scarlet pouts in frustration.

INT. GANGSTER HIDEOUT - NIGHT

Several gangsters sit around a table in the backroom of a
dark warehouse. They play poker and smoke cigars. BIG
LOU -- 40's, large, slicked-back hair -- sits with JOEY
STINKEYE, ANTONIO THE MOUTH, and FRANK SLAPNUTS.

                    FRANK SLAPNUTS
          This new mayor talks a big game.

                    JOEY STINKEYE
          Yeah, no one here better be
          stealing cakes.

                    FRANK SLAPNUTS
          Are you a moron?

Joey Stinkeye doesn't get it. Antonio looks to Big Lou.

                    ANTONIO
          Big Lou, what are we going to do
          now that Billie got popped?

Big Lou reclines in his seat.

                    BIG LOU
          We need to see how serious he is.
          Let's lay low for a bit.

                    FRANK SLAPNUTS
          How are we going to collect our
          money with a bounty on our heads?

                    BIG LOU
          We won't collect.

                    ANTONIO
          But with all due respect --

                    BIG LOU
          We will find some fresh blood to
          collect. We will offer them money.
          They know nothing. If they get
          caught, they won't be able to prove
          anything.

Big Lou stands up from the table.

                    FRANK SLAPNUTS
          Do you think this new mayor can be
          bought?

                    BIG LOU
          Doesn't seem like it. But he can
          be intimidated.

                    FRANK SLAPNUTS
          Mayor Billie was a huge asset. He
          sure knew how to make a deal. We
          all benefited.

                    BIG LOU
          Regrettably, someone here thought
          they could benefit the most, and
          cut their own deal. And now Mayor
          Billie is in the slammer.

Antonio, Frank and Joey Stinkeye sit silently. Then Big
Lou pulls a pistol! BANG!

Joey Stinkeye's body tumbles backward over the chair.

                    BIG LOU
          He folds.

INT. KIMMY'S HOUSE, LIVING ROOM - NIGHT

Bryan, Vanessa and Kimmy eat dinner together.

                    KIMMY
          Dad, why do you hate the circus?

                    BRYAN
          Kimmy, I don't hate the circus.
          It's just... those people... they
          are all criminals.

                    KIMMY
          The fat clown just stole a birthday
          cake. It's not a big deal.

                    BRYAN
          It doesn't matter what he stole,
          honey. He stole. Theft is wrong.

                    KIMMY
          Maybe he was just hungry.

                    BRYAN
          Have you seen how fat he is?

                    VANESSA
          Must we talk about this?

An awkward silence hangs in the air.

                    KIMMY
          I want to go to the circus.

                    BRYAN
          No.

                    KIMMY
          Why not?

                    BRYAN
          It's dangerous! Those people are
          crooks. And there are wild animals.

                    KIMMY
          I want to see it!

                    BRYAN
          No!

Kimmy conjures up some sad puppy dog eyes.

                    KIMMY
          Pleeease!

                    BRYAN
          I said no! There's nothing to see!
          The circus and those hooligans will
          soon be gone.

                    KIMMY
          I want to see a man get shot out of
          a cannon.

                    BRYAN
          I'll tell you what. When we arrest
          Big Lou, we'll shoot him out of a
          cannon.

Kimmy slumps back, discouraged.

                    KIMMY
          May I be excused?

                    VANESSA
          Of course, sweetheart.

Kimmy gets up and runs off into another room.

                    VANESSA
          What's the harm in letting her go?

INT. KIMMY'S HOUSE, KIMMY'S BEDROOM - NIGHT

Kimmy is sitting on her bed, iPad in hand. She watches a
YouTube video of old circus footage. She is entranced.

A message pops up on his computer screen. It
reads: "GINGER: Hey Kimmy, story bout ur dad. check <u>this
out</u>."

Kimmy taps the link. A local news website loads. A
video shows Yolanda Scarlet reporting from the inauguration.

                    SCARLET
          Today, Mayor Bryan Scott was sworn
          in, replacing disgraced former
          Mayor Bill Swine, who was found
          guilty of doing business with mob
          leader Big Lou. However, the
          mayor's amateurism and political
          inexperience embarrassed him today
          as he was more focused on clowns
          than criminals.

GLASS SHATTERS! Kimmy is startled.

INT. KIMMY'S HOUSE, LIVING ROOM - NIGHT

Kimmy rushes down the stairs to find her dad inspecting a
ROCK in the living room; it has been thrown through the
window.

EXT. KIMMY'S HOUSE - NIGHT

Bryan bursts out of the front door. TIRES SQUEAL.

Bryan watches helplessly as A GANGSTER CAR SPEEDS AWAY.

INT. KIMMY'S HOUSE, LIVING ROOM - MOMENTS LATER

Bryan and Sheriff Bob stand at the dining table, looking at
the stone. Off to the side, Vanessa stands with Kimmy.
Other uniformed officers inspect the house.

                    SHERIFF BOB
          This is a message from Big Lou.

                    BRYAN
          Or... it could be the circus folk.

Everyone looks at Bryan as if he were an idiot.

                    BRYAN
          Well, we shouldn't jump to
          conclusions!

                    KIMMY
          If the circus people wanted to
          fight you, they'd throw a pie in
          your face.

                    BRYAN
          Speaking of which, we need to make
          that illegal.

Sheriff Bob snaps his fingers to get Bryan's attention.

                    SHERIFF BOB
          Sir, the circus folk have no
          violent history. This is the
          gangsters. Plain and simple.

Vanessa gestures toward the rock.

                    VANESSA
          These are the criminals you need to
          worry about.

EXT. SCHOOLYARD - DAY

Kimmy runs across the schoolyard to where Jacob and Ginger
-- also a 9 year-old girl -- are hanging out. Ginger plays
on her smartphone.

                    KIMMY
          Ginger, Jacob! Have you guys ever
          been to the circus?

                    GINGER
          Nah.

                    KIMMY
          Want to go?

                    GINGER
          To the circus? Hashtag lame.

Ginger bangs away on the smartphone.

                    KIMMY
          Don't you want to see where the fat
          clown comes from?

                    JACOB
          I hope that fat clown shows up at
          my next birthday party.

                    KIMMY
          My dad was pissed that he showed up
          at my party. Now he wants to close
          down the circus.

Kimmy glances at Ginger, who is busy on her phone.

                    KIMMY
          Ginger, are you listening?

                    GINGER
          Hashtag circus. Hashtag fat
          clowns. Hashtag not going.

                    KIMMY
          Can I tell my dad I'm going to your
          house for a sleepover?

For the first time, Ginger stops playing with the phone.

                    GINGER
          Your dad is the mayor now. Like, I
          don't wanna be on his bad side.

                    KIMMY
          Well, if you don't blog about it,
          he won't know!

Jacob awkwardly raises his hand.

                    JACOB
          Uh, I vote we go.

Ginger gives Jacob a disapproving looks, shakes her head,
and walks away.

INT. MAYOR'S OFFICE - DAY

Bryan sits behind his desk. He fiddles with a pen. Sheriff
Bob sits across from him, as does another man in a suit, MR.
MUDWORD -- 50's, stuffy, all business.

                    BRYAN
          What do you mean there's nothing?

                    SHERIFF BOB
          I can't arrest them for being a
          circus.

                    BRYAN
          What's the point of having laws if
          no one breaks them?!
               (beat)
          Can we tie them to Big Lou or any
          mob money?

                    SHERIFF BOB
          There's an open loan from the bank.
          Nothing suspicious.

Bryan taps the pen, lost in thought.

                    SHERIFF BOB
          Mr. Mayor, shouldn't we focus on
          going after Big Lou and not
          shutting down some stupid circus?

                    BRYAN
          Look, we'll get to Big Lou, but
          first, we need to deal with these
          circus folk.

                    SHERIFF BOB
          Is this because he stole your
          daughter's birthday cake?

                    BRYAN
              (ignoring the question)
          I want to show the gangsters we
          mean business.

                    SHERIFF BOB
          The gangsters vandalized your home.
          That's worse than stolen cake.

Bryan points the pen at the other man.

                    BRYAN
          Mr. Mudword, have you had a chance
          to look at the circus property?

                    MUDWORD
          Aye. It is an attractive piece of
          property. Ripe for development.

                    BRYAN
          You're interested, then?

                    MUDWORD
          It is an investment that my firm
          would gladly consider.

                    BRYAN
          Excellent!

Bryan picks up his phone.

                    BRYAN
          Get me the chief loan officer at
          the Chiffon Ridge Savings Bank.

INT. CIRCUS TENT, BACKSTAGE - DAY

The performers prepare for a show. Tubby tries to pin
a squirting flower on his lapel. Alazander walks up beside
him with a newspaper in hand.

                    ALAZANDER
          Looks like you've stolen the wrong
          cake this time.

Pudgey, having overheard this, looks over with concern.
Alazander unrolls the newspaper for Tubby to see.

The headline reads: "Mayor to Crack Down on Circus Crime."

                    ALAZANDER
          The new mayor doesn't like that you
          stole his daughter's cake.

Tubby is at a loss for words. Pudgey steps closer.

                    PUDGEY
          Tubby, you've got to be careful.

                    ALAZANDER
          I must say that I agree with the
          mayor. The crime in this town is
          appalling.

Alazander turns quickly and begins to walk away. He stops
and looks back to add:

                    ALAZANDER
          Prison may be good for you. You
          might lose a few pounds.

Alazander exits.

                    PUDGEY
          Don't let him get to you. We've
          got a big performance tonight.
          There are actually children in the
          audience.

Tubby's face lights up with joy.

                    MISS ROLLY
                 (in Tubby's head)
          Strike while the oven is hot.

Tubby leaps up from his chair.

                    TUBBY
          Everyone! Gather round!

All of the performers form a circle around Tubby.

                    TUBBY
          Not only do we have an audience
          tonight, but children have come to
          see the show! If we amaze these
          kids, they'll tell their friends
          and more and more children will
          come. Let's put on the best damn
          show this circus has ever seen!
          This is a perfect opportunity to
          generate some excitement!

There are a few scattered cheers.

                    ALAZANDER (O.C.)
          This _is_ a perfect opportunity.

The crowd of performers parts. Alazander re-enters along
with some new performers and Pepper.

                    ALAZANDER (CONT'D)
          A perfect opportunity to try
          something new.

                    TUBBY
          Who are all these people?

                    ALAZANDER
          Allow me to introduce
          some extraordinarily talented
          friends of mine. First, this is
          Ted, our new lighting director.

TED -- short, shoddy-looking, wearing a baseball cap --
gives a little wave.

                    TED
          What's up!

                    ALAZANDER
          Ted has worked out some new
          lighting cues that are
          breathtaking. The laser-lights
          will, undoubtedly, pump up the
          crowd.

Tubby scoffs.

                    TUBBY
          We _have_ lights.

                    ALAZANDER
          I doubt that they're all on
          upstairs.

Tubby is confused.

Alazander gestures to a tall, skinny man dressed in a
skin-tight black outfit.

                    ALAZANDER
          And this is Vlad. With his team,
          he will be doing the new acrobatic
          routines.

VLAD smiles broadly and takes a small bow.

                    VLAD
          It will be my pleasure to
          revitalize this show.

A mostly naked woman enters.

                    ALAZANDER
          And this is Zelda.

                    TUBBY
          You actually hired a stripper?
          There are children in the audience!

                    ALAZANDER
          Burlesque. There's a difference.

ZELDA -- early 20's, thin, scantily-clad -- eyes Tubby from
top to bottom.

                    ZELDA
          My, there is a lot of you to love.

Pudgey throws Zelda an angry look.

Tubby is fuming. He turns to Pepper.

                    TUBBY
          You approve of this?

Pepper hesitates, goes to speak, but is cut off:

                    ALAZANDER
          The ringmaster has given
          me authority to revitalize the
          show. We will have revamped visual
          effects, acrobats, and... more
          magic!

Suddenly, there are BANGS, FLASHES OF LIGHT, and SMOKE!

                    TUBBY
          We don't need more magic, Pepper!

                    ALAZANDER
          You should know that the ringmaster
          did forbid me one trick. I
          suggested that we make the fat
          clown disappear. Forever.

                    TUBBY
          Pepper, can I talk to you
          privately?

Pepper nods and the two walk to a corner of the room. Pepper
raises a hand before Tubby can speak.

                    PEPPER
          I know what you are going to say,
          but Alazander is right. We must
          explore other options.

Before Tubby can protest, Pepper puts on his top hat and
turns back to face all the performers.

                    PEPPER
          Have a fabulous show, everyone!

INT. CIRCUS TENT - NIGHT

The show is in full-swing. Kimmy, Ginger, and Jacob are
seated alone in the bleachers.

                    GINGER
          You do realize we are the only
          people here?

Tubby enters the main stage and starts to shoot water at
other performers from his flower lapel.

Kimmy is excited to see Tubby. She points Ginger and Jacob
to the clown.

                    KIMMY
          That's him! That's the fat
          clown from my party!

Ginger snaps a photo of Tubby on her phone.

                    GINGER
          I don't want to even post this.
          It's embarrassing.
               (to Kimmy)
          I can't believe you dragged me
          here.

                    JACOB
               (insincere)
          I think it's cool.

Up in the catwalks, Alazander emerges from the shadows and
whispers into Ted's ear.

On stage, Tubby continues to chase the other performers.
Then the laser-lights start. Tubby is blinded. He motions
that he cannot see. Ted dutifully follows Tubby with one of
the lights.

30.

Alazander slips off into the shadows of the catwalk.

Tubby attempts to hit other performers with his
water-spitting flower, but misses wildly.

                    PERFORMER #1
          What's that matter with you?

                    TUBBY
          The laser-lights, they're blinding
          me! I can't see!

Tubby loses his footing and falls off the platform and onto
his back.

Performer #2 tries to help him up, but Tubby is too heavy
and Performer #2 just falls on top of Tubby.

A light shines on Pepper, standing a top a pillar.

                    PEPPER
          Well, let's just move on to Vlad
          and the Amazing Air Dancers!

Tubby is furious. Kimmy and Jacob laugh. Ginger rolls her
eyes.

                    JACOB
          Look, he's so fat, he can't get up!

Tubby rolls on the floor like a turtle on its back, yelling
at the top of his lungs.

                    TUBBY
          No! Cannon shot is next!

Pepper is caught off guard.

                    PEPPER
          Be quiet! Vlad and the Amazing Air
          Dancers are next!

Vlad and his acrobats start their show.

Performer #3 tries to help Tubby up, but is unsuccessful.
Alazander slowly walks up alongside Tubby and stares down at
him.

                    TUBBY
          Your friends are ruining our show!

                    ALAZANDER
          Ordinarily, I'd say your gross
          physique ruins the show. But right
          now, it's proving useful in keeping
          you out of the show.

Tubby is furious and finds the strength to jump up to
his feet. He gives Alazander a big shove and a slap in the
face.

Alazander falls backwards against the door of the tiger
cage. The cage door flips open and the TIGER rushes out.

The tiger ROARS!

Pepper is visibly shaken, but quickly gains his composure.

                    PEPPER
                 (improvising)
          Uh, and now, Billy our Tiger-Tamer!

No one comes on stage. Pepper looks around nervously, his
head on a swivel.

                    PEPPER
                 (to self)
          Where is Billy?

Ginger records video on his smartphone.

                    GINGER
          Now, this might get some likes.
                 (calling to tiger)
          Hey, over here!

The tiger catches sight of the children and moves in their
direction.

                    JACOB
          Shut up, don't call him over!

                    GINGER
          I want a tiger selfie.

                    KIMMY
          Is anyone else scared?

Catching Kimmy's worried look, Jacob sits up straight to
look tough.

                    JACOB
          No. It's only a tiger.

The tiger draws nearer.

32.

                    KIMMY
          I don't like this. Why is he still
          coming this way?

The tiger advances.

                    JACOB
          Maybe we should get out of here...

The tiger crouches down, ready to pounce.

                    KIMMY
          Run!

Kimmy and Jacob run!

Ginger, trying to position herself to take a selfie with the
tiger, stays behind. Jacob runs back and grabs her by the
arm and pulls her away.

The tiger leaps into the audience!

HONK! HONK! HONK!

Tubby wildly honks his clown nose to distract the tiger. The
tiger's attention is caught.

                    TUBBY
          Over here!

The tiger turns and studies Tubby. It eyes the clown for a
moment and then charges at him.

Tubby slips off one of his giant clown shoes and readies it
like a baseball bat.

The tiger leaps at him! Tubby WHACKS it with the shoe.

The tiger is disoriented momentarily. Tubby runs into the
cage and the tiger follows. They circle one another. Tubby
uses his other shoe to protect himself from the tiger's
swipes.

Tubby lowers the shoe and uses his lapel flower to squirt
water at the tiger. The tiger is repulsed by the water.

Tubby makes an escape from the cage. The Bearded Lady and
some other performers rush over and seal the cage.

INT. CIRCUS TENT, BACKSTAGE - NIGHT

                    PEPPER
          Are you both complete idiots?

Pepper paces before Tubby and Alazander. He is fuming.

                    TUBBY
          But, he --

                    PEPPER
          I do not want to hear it! If that
          tiger had gotten a hold of those
          kids --

                    ALAZANDER
          Perhaps if the fat clown was more
          agile.

                    PEPPER
          Enough! Both of you, go home.

Pepper turns to find the Bearded Lady approaching.

                    BEARDED LADY
          Pepper, there's a man here to see
          you.

                    PEPPER
          Great. Now what?

Pepper moans and exits.

Tubby walks over toward the exit of the tent and sees Pepper
shake hands with a MAN IN A SUIT.

Pudgey walks up alongside Tubby.

                    PUDGEY
          Who do you reckon he is?

                    TUBBY
          Dunno, but it doesn't look good.

EXT. CIRCUS GROUNDS - NIGHT

Tubby walks, lost in thought. He eyes the SCATTERED JUNK
everywhere. Tubby lowers his head in sadness.

Then, Tubby is startled. Kimmy emerges from between two
trailers.

                    KIMMY
              (timidly)
          Hello.

                    TUBBY
          Hi...

Tubby looks around, searching for clues about why this kid
is here.

                    KIMMY
          I was at the show today. I really
          enjoyed it. Except for when the
          tiger tried to eat me.

                    TUBBY
          You're lucky. The show's
          ordinarily not that interactive.

                    KIMMY
          My name is Kimmy.

                    TUBBY
          They call me Tubby.

                    KIMMY
          You're the fat clown who steals
          birthday cakes.

Tubby lowers his head.

                    TUBBY
          I'm not going to be able to do that
          anymore. Our new mayor doesn't
          like it when I do that.

                    KIMMY
          My dad is the new mayor.

Worry fills Tubby's face.

                    TUBBY
          I will repay him for the birthday
          cake! I promise.

                    KIMMY
          It was funny! My friends say I had
          the coolest party all year.

                    TUBBY
          Your dad says I'm a criminal.

                    KIMMY
          He doesn't like people who break
          the rules.

Tubby surveys the area again.

                    TUBBY
          Your dad doesn't know that you're
          here, does he?

                    KIMMY
          He thinks I'm at a friend's house.

                    TUBBY
          You're not going to turn me in, are
          you?

                    KIMMY
          No! I want repay the favor.

                    TUBBY
          What do you mean?

                    KIMMY
          I'm going to tell everyone at
          school to come see the circus.

Tubby is at a loss for words.

                    TUBBY
          You'd do that for me?

                    KIMMY
          Of course. You made my birthday
          party the best one yet! All my
          friends loved it.

Tubby smiles.

                    TUBBY
          It's getting late. How are you
          getting home?

                    KIMMY
          I'll walk back to my friend's
          house.

                    TUBBY
          Let me get you a ride.

36.

EXT. EDGE OF CIRCUS GROUNDS - NIGHT

Tubby walks Kimmy to the edge of the circus grounds. Raoul
and his taxi cab are waiting.

                    RAOUL
          Tubby, my friend! What? No
          birthday cake today? You're gonna
          starve!

                    TUBBY
          Not this time. I need you to take
          my friend here home.

                    RAOUL
          Of course, of course. Anything for
          you. Come on, young lady.

Tubby holds the door open as Kimmy climbs in.

                    KIMMY
          Don't worry. I'll help you make
          the circus cool again.

Tubby shuts the door and the cab drives off.

INT. PEPPER'S TRAILER - NIGHT

Pepper pours himself a brandy. There is a knock at the
door.

                    PEPPER
          Come in!

Tubby struggles to make his way through the doorway. The
trailer begins to shake wildly.

                    PEPPER
          Stop it! I'll come outside.

EXT. CIRCUS GROUNDS - NIGHT

Pepper emerges from the trailer.

                    TUBBY
          Pepper, I have great news. One of
          the kids in the audience found me.
          She said that she loved the show
          and she's going to tell all her
          friends to come.

                    PEPPER
          It's too late for that.

                    TUBBY
          What do you mean?

                    PEPPER
          Some jackass from the bank came to
          visit me after the show. They're
          calling in the loans I've taken
          out. I've got 30 days to pay them
          back. I don't have the money. Not
          even close.

                    TUBBY
          We'll sell more tickets.

                    PEPPER
          To who?

                    TUBBY
          Kimmy's friends. We'll get more
          kids to come. Even if it means
          keeping the stupid acrobats and
          light show.

                    PEPPER
          Several businessmen have expressed
          interest in buying the circus. I've
          chased them away for a while,
          but --

                    TUBBY
          What do businessmen know about
          running a circus?

Pepper chuckles.

                    PEPPER
          No one will run the circus. The
          circus will close and the land will
          be developed into a high rise.

                    TUBBY
          No. I won't allow it!

Pepper is startled by Tubby's defiance.

                    TUBBY (CONT'D)
          The circus is my home. It's home
          for many of us. You can't sell it!

Pepper sighs.

                    PEPPER
          The bank is playing hard ball. What
          can I do but pay off the debts and
          retire somewhere quiet to live out
          the rest of my days?

                    TUBBY
          There's still time.

                    PEPPER
          I'm an old man. I'll tell you this
          though: I don't have any regrets
          about having tried to make this
          work.

Pepper takes a swig of his brandy.

                    PEPPER
          I only regret one thing: I never
          put on a show of a lifetime.

                    TUBBY
          I'll come up with the money to save
          the circus. Just you watch.

                    PEPPER
          Tubby. We only have 30 days. Then,
          they foreclose. We would need a
          miracle.

                    TUBBY
          I can whip up a miracle!
               (beat)
          Mmm. Miracle Whip...

Pepper shakes his head in disgust.

INT. SCHOOL, CAFETERIA - DAY

Kimmy sits among a group of kids.

                    KIMMY
          There's a tiger, acrobats, and a
          bearded woman.

                    GIRL #1
          That's impossible. Women don't
          grow beards.

                    KIMMY
          This one has.

                    BOY #1
          So has our history teacher.

                    KIMMY
          And guess who works there?

The kids look at one another; no one has an answer.

                    KIMMY
          The fat clown who steals birthday
          cakes!

                    BOY #2
          No way!

                    KIMMY
          Yeah. We're actually friends now.

                    BOY #2
          No way! Sweet!

                    HISTORY TEACHER (O.C.)
          Excuse me.

The kids look up to see the HISTORY TEACHER, sporting some
facial hair, standing over them. She speaks in a deep,
raspy voice.

                    HISTORY TEACHER
          Please keep your voices down.

The history teacher walks off.

Jacob approaches and sheepishly taps Kimmy on the shoulder.

                    JACOB
          Can I talk to you? In private?

                    KIMMY
          Sure.

Kimmy gets up and follows Jacob. As she does, she is teased
by the children:

                    BOY #3
          Ooh, Kimmy's got a boyfriend!

They are a good distance away when Jacob stops and faces
her.

                    JACOB
          My birthday is next week. I was
          hoping you could ask the fat clown
                    (MORE)

40.

                    JACOB (cont'd)
          to make sure he steals my birthday
          cake.

Kimmy grins.

                    KIMMY
          I can do that.

INT. TUBBY'S TRAILER - NIGHT

Tubby draws on large sheets of poster board. He has written
out statements such as "Come See the Circus - It's Groovy"
or "Clowns are Cool."

He reaches for a doughnut, one of many on a nearby plate.

There is a KNOCK on the door.

                    TUBBY
          Come in!

Kimmy enters.

                    KIMMY
          Hi, Tubby.

Tubby is surprised.

                    TUBBY
          You again?

                    KIMMY
          Yeah, I have a question for you...

She is distracted by the posters.

                    KIMMY
          What are you doing?

                    TUBBY
          Making posters. Eating doughnuts.

Kimmy reads the posters.

                    KIMMY
          You know, people don't really say
          "groovy" anymore.

                    TUBBY
          Oh, so you're going to start trying
          to change the circus too?

                    KIMMY
          Just sayin'.

Kimmy eyes the plate full of doughnuts.

                    KIMMY
          Are you really going to eat all
          those doughnuts?

                    TUBBY
          Brain food.

                    KIMMY
          Oh.

                    TUBBY
          You don't want any, do you?

                    KIMMY
          No.

                    TUBBY
          Good, because I'm starving!

Kimmy picks up one of the posters.

                    KIMMY
          What are you doing with these?

                    TUBBY
          It's called marketing. The circus
          needs to advertise. Not enough
          people are coming to see the show.

                    KIMMY
          I can help!

                    TUBBY
          Grab a marker, a poster board and
          join the party!

Kimmy looks at Tubby incredulously. Tubby reluctantly grabs
the plate of doughnuts and extends them to Kimmy.

                    TUBBY
          Fine. Grab a doughnut. Only one,
          though!

Kimmy smiles and takes a doughnut.

42.

EXT. SUBURBAN STREETS - DAY

Tubby and Kimmy walk down a street. Kimmy holds a stack of
posters.

                    KIMMY
          What made you join the circus?

Tubby takes a poster from Kimmy and staples it to a
telephone pole.

                    TUBBY
          It's the only place I fit in.

                    KIMMY
          You felt welcomed there?

                    TUBBY
          No, the circus tent is big and has
          large doors.

They arrive at the next telephone pole and Tubby takes
another poster to hang.

                    KIMMY
          But why not another job?

                    TUBBY
          When I was your age, the circus was
          a place of wonder and escape. It
          was exciting and majestic. Like a
          chocolate blackout cake. I never
          wanted to do anything else.

Tubby takes another poster and hangs it up.

Across the street, A MAN ON A BENCH READS A NEWSPAPER.

He lowers the newspaper to reveal that it is Alazander. He
spies on the clown and girl. Slyly, he raises the newspaper
to hide again.

INT. TUBBY'S TRAILER - DAY

Tubby shows Kimmy some old, faded photographs of the circus.

                    TUBBY
          Back in the good old days, we could
          pack the entire audience. We
          actually sold out.

Kimmy holds a picture of a younger Tubby.

                    KIMMY
          You used to be... eh, younger.

                    TUBBY
          And thinner! A trim 350 pounds!

Tubby takes a bite of cannoli.

                    KIMMY
          Right... So, a friend of mine is
          having a birthday party next week.
          His name is Jacob. Can you come
          steal his birthday cake?

Tubby shoves some tiramisu into his mouth.

                    TUBBY
          Say no more! I'm there!

                    KIMMY
          Thanks Tubby. I'd better get
          going before my parents worry about
          me.

                    TUBBY
          Thanks for your help today. I hope
          these posters work.

Tubby looks over to where a calendar hangs on the wall. Two
days have red X's through them.

                    TUBBY (CONT'D)
          There's only 28 days until the bank
          forecloses.

                    KIMMY
          It's too bad we don't have time to
          put posters all over the country.
          It'd be nice to attract some
          tourists.

                    TUBBY
          I don't think Pepper has money for
          national advertising.

                    KIMMY
          Bye, Tubby.

Kimmy exits while Tubby finishes the tiramisu.

A few seconds later, Kimmy bursts back into the room!

                    KIMMY
          I have a great idea!

INT. TUBBY'S TRAILER - MOMENTS LATER

An episode of "Finding Bigfoot" plays on Tubby's television.

                    KIMMY
          See! These crazy people spend
          their time in the woods looking for
          Bigfoot!

Tubby doesn't follow.

                    KIMMY (CONT'D)
          Everyone in our town knows who you
          are, but if we make you an internet
          sensation, we'll attract people
          from around the country! They'll
          come to see you!

Tubby leans back on his sofa, a bowl of popcorn in hand.

                    TUBBY
          You want to make a TV show about
          me?

                    KIMMY
          A web series, but yeah. We take
          your story, create a folklore like
          Big Foot, and get national
          attention. People will come to the
          circus for a chance to see you in
          person!

Tubby considers this.

                    TUBBY
          Like Big Foot, huh?
               (beat)
          We're not calling this Big Belly.

                    KIMMY
          No, no. We can call it... "Chasing
          Tubby"

EXT. TUBBY'S TRAILER - DAY

Alazander creepily listens through an open window of Tubby's
trailer.

EXT. JACOB'S HOUSE, BACKYARD - DAY

Jacob's birthday party is underway. Ginger fusses with her smartphone. Jacob runs up alongside Kimmy.

                    JACOB
          He's coming, right? I think my mom
          is going to bring out the cake
          soon.

                    KIMMY
          Yeah, he said he'll be here.

                    JACOB
          He better! My mom bought two
          cakes. You're the best!

Jacob excitedly runs off.

                    KIMMY
          You better show up, you fat fool.

Kimmy turns to Ginger.

                    KIMMY
          Remember, get a picture. Then
          tweet it with #chasingtubby.

                    GINGER
          This is so lame.

                    KIMMY
          You've got like a billion
          followers. We need this.

Jacob's mom emerges from within the house, cake in hand.

                    JACOB'S MOM
          Come on everyone! It's cake time!

The entire party moves to encircle the patio table where Jacob is seated. Kimmy pushes her way to the front of the crowd and readies her phone.

Jacob looks around. Concern fills his face. He looks at Kimmy who replies with a shrug.

                    JACOB'S MOM
          Make a wish, darling.

                    JACOB
          Just a minute.

Jacob gives Kimmy an angry look. Kimmy shakes her head.

                         JACOB'S MOM
               Honey?

Jacob resigns himself to the fact that Tubby isn't coming.
He takes a deep breathe.

Kimmy hits record on her phone.

Before Jacob can blow out the candles, THE CAKE IS SNATCHED!

COMMOTION ensues! The parents are bewildered. The kids
laugh hysterically.

Kimmy chases Tubby frantically, trying to keep him in frame
of the camera.

ON GINGER'S PHONE, she tweets a photo of Tubby running with
the cake. Under it: "#chasingtubby"

INT. JACOB'S HOUSE - DAY

Tubby runs through the house, shoving cake in his face as he
goes.

                          KIMMY
               Keep going! Keep going!

Tubby knocks over a lamp and a chair, but barrels toward the
front door.

EXT. SUBURBAN STREET - DAY

Tubby bursts onto the front lawn. He HONKS his clown nose.

Down the block, RAOUL'S TAXI CAB turns the corner.

Tubby waves to Raoul. Then, he is KNOCKED TO THE GROUND!

Kimmy exits the house and sees that TWO POLICE OFFICERS have
tackled Tubby.

                          TUBBY
               No! No!

Half of the birthday cake lay splattered on the sidewalk.

Raoul makes a U-turn and drives away from the house.

Kimmy, Jacob, Jacob's parents, Ginger, and the other
guests gather on the front lawn.

                    TUBBY
          Hey, what's the big idea?

                    OFFICER #1
          C'mon, get up.

The officer tries to pull him up, without success.

                    OFFICER #1
          Sir, give me your hand.

Tubby complies. The officer falls down onto Tubby. The
spectators laugh. The officers are not amused.

                    OFFICER #2
          I'll help you.

Each officer takes one of Tubby's arms. They try to lift
him, but fail.

The officers take a step back and catch their breath.

                    OFFICER #1
          We're gonna need backup.

Officer #2 grabs his walky-talky.

                    OFFICER #2
          This is 1L-19. We got an
          eleven-ninety-two.

                    DISPATCHER
            (over radio)
          Ten-four. We have a fat clown who
          can't be lifted. Nearby units
          report.

                    TUBBY
          What did I do?

                    OFFICER #1
          Sir, you've been caught red-nosed
          stealing a birthday cake.

                    TUBBY
          Are you profiling me because I'm
          fat?

                    OFFICER #2
          You're going to do some serious
          time for this one.

48.

                    TUBBY
          Clown lives matter!

                    JACOB (O.C.)
          No!

Startled, the officers spin to face Jacob.

                    JACOB
          You can't arrest him! I invited
          him to my party!

Jacob begins to cry. The officers look at one another.

Jacob's mom puts her arms around Jacob and comforts him.

                    JACOB'S MOM
          It's okay, honey.

                    JACOB
          I don't want Tubby to go to jail!

Two patrol cars arrive with four more officers.

                    JACOB
          Don't take him! Don't take him!

The officers gather around Tubby and, with great effort, get
him back on his feet.

                    TUBBY
          I guess they don't have fitness
          tests for you guys anymore.

Officer #1 TASERS Tubby, but it has little effect.

                    TUBBY
          Oh, that tickles!

The officers are perplexed.

                    OFFICER #2
          Is that thing working?

Officer #1 TASERS him again. Nothing but a tickle.

                    OFFICER #1
          He must have too much blubber!

Kimmy steps forward.

                    KIMMY
          I don't think you want to arrest
          this man.

The officers look at one another, chuckling.

                    OFFICER #1
          And why is that, little lady?

                    KIMMY
          My dad's the mayor and this clown
          is a friend of mine.

The officers' chuckling quickly stops. Now they are
uncertain.

                    OFFICER #1
          But, your dad hates clowns.

                    KIMMY
          Do you want me to tell him how you
          guys ruined a little boy's birthday
          party?

Officer #1 approaches Jacob's mom.

                    OFFICER #1
          Ma'am, do you want to press
          charges?

Jacob, hysterical and crying, looks up to his mom. They
make eye contact.

                    JACOB
          Mom, I asked him to come!

Jacob and his mom lock eyes.

                    OFFICER #1
          Ma'am?

                    JACOB'S MOM
          No. I do not.

                    OFFICER #1
          Okay, then...

Officer #1 turns to face the other officers.

                    OFFICER #1
          Right. We're out of here.

50.

                    KIMMY
          Hey, how did you know he would be
          here?

                    OFFICER #1
          An anonymous tip.

The officers scatter and return to their vehicles.

Tubby catches a quick glimpse of Alazander down the block,
hiding behind a tree, peaking out to see the action. He
quickly vanishes is a FLASH OF SMOKE.

As the patrol cars drive off, Kimmy approaches Tubby. She
holds up her smartphone.

                    KIMMY
          We got some great stuff!

Tubby looks at the splattered cake on the pavement, reaches
down and scrapes off a piece. He eats it.

Kimmy watches him in disbelief.

INT. MAYOR'S OFFICE - DAY

                    BRYAN
          I want their badges!

Bryan is fuming. He paces behind his desk.   Sheriff Bob
stands on the opposite side of the desk.

                    SHERIFF BOB
          The boy was very upset. He had
          wished for the clown to show up.

                    BRYAN
          Oh, so we shouldn't enforce the law
          because a little brat threw a
          tantrum?

                    SHERIFF BOB
          The boy's mother declined to press
          charges.

                    BRYAN
          Maybe we should let murderers walk
          free then? After all, their
          victims don't have the ability to
          press charges!

Bryan takes a deep breath and gazes out the office window.

                    SHERIFF BOB
               (hesitantly)
          There's more.

                    BRYAN
          What?

                    SHERIFF BOB
          Your daughter was the party. She
          told the officers you wouldn't want
          the clown arrested. She said the
          clown is her friend.

Rage fills Bryan's eyes.

INT. KIMMY'S HOUSE, KIMMY'S BEDROOM - NIGHT

Kimmy is re-watching the footage from Jacob's party on her
laptop.

Bryan bursts into Kimmy's bedroom.

                    BRYAN
          My job doesn't give you the right
          to special treatment from the
          police. Is that clear, missy?

                    KIMMY
          What special treatment?

                    BRYAN
          You shouldn't be friends with that
          clown!

                    KIMMY
          Why not?

Bryan hesitates.

                    BRYAN
          You might get fat!

                    KIMMY
          That's a stupid reason.

                    BRYAN
          You're grounded for a month!

                    KIMMY
          That's unfair!

                    BRYAN
          Unfair?   There are laws.

                    KIMMY
          And what "law" did I break?

                    BRYAN
          Disloyalty to me and my agenda as
          mayor of this town. And it could
          be worse. I could lock you up for
          aiding and abetting a criminal.

Bryan exits and slams the door behind him.

INT. ALAZANDER'S TRAILER - NIGHT

The inside of the trailer looks like a fun house. There are
many mirrors and props.

Alazander and Tubby stand face-to-face.

                    ALAZANDER
          Even in the thin mirror, you still
          look fat.

                    TUBBY
          Yeah, well you look fat in that
          mirror.

                    ALAZANDER
          That's the fat mirror.
          Incidentally, it protrudes your...
          physique... beyond its own
          boundaries. Exceptional.

                    TUBBY
          Why did you tip off the police?

                    ALAZANDER
          About what?

                    TUBBY
          I saw you at the party.

Alazander walks over to the kitchen area where he tends to a
cauldron of smoking green liquid.

                    ALAZANDER
          You and the girl cannot save the
          circus. Might I remind you that
          the girl's own father wants to see
          the circus put out of business.

                    TUBBY
          Why are we working against one
          another?

                    ALAZANDER
          I'm sorry. Did you want help
          hanging your ridiculous posters?

                    TUBBY
          Hey, at least I'm trying to help.

                    ALAZANDER
          No one wants to see the circus as
          it is. A new show means new money.
          The sooner we adapt, the sooner we
          can bring in new investors and pay
          off the bank.

Tubby turns to leave.

                    ALAZANDER
          I understand that you and the girl
          intend to use video to create some
          interest in you, and by extension,
          the circus.

Tubby turns back to Alazander, surprised.

                    TUBBY
          How do you know that?

                    ALAZANDER
          I would like to show you a little
          video of my own.

Alazander waves his arms. There is a FLASH OF LIGHT and A
TELEVISION APPEARS.

Alazander picks up a remote. Grainy footage of Kimmy and
her friends at the circus appears on-screen.

                    ALAZANDER
          This is the security footage from
          the day that the tiger attacked the
          mayor's daughter.

The footage shows the tiger leaping into the seats.

                    ALAZANDER (CONT'D)
          It would be a pity if this ended up
          in the hands of a fearless reporter
          like Miss Yolanda Scarlet. Noses
          would, undoubtedly, need to roll.
                    (MORE)

54.

                    ALAZANDER (CONT'D)
          As it so happens, Miss Scarlet is
          an old friend of mine.

Tubby takes several steps toward Alazander, until they are
inches apart.

                    TUBBY
          We should be working together. You
          could ask Miss Scarlet to promote
          the circus, the web series, do a
          profile piece on Pepper's life --

                    ALAZANDER
          I won't ask her to risk her
          journalistic integrity to raise
          money.

                    TUBBY
          Yeah? Well, we're also not
          changing the show. Or firing our
          oldest performers.

                    ALAZANDER
          Is this what Pudgey sees in you?
          Hopeless idealism?

Tubby quickly squeezes his flower lapel and squirts water
into Alazander's face.

Tubby exits.

EXT. CIRCUS GROUNDS - NIGHT

Pudgey is walking the grounds, humming a melody to herself.

She sees Tubby off in the distance, fuming mad.

Alazander exits his trailer, wiping water from his face.
He sidles up beside Pudgey.

                    PUDGEY
          What did you do to him now?

                    ALAZANDER
          I'm trying to help him see the
          obvious. If he cannot accept the
          ways things will be, he'll be
          forced to leave.

                    PUDGEY
          I will leave with him.

Alazander scoffs.

                    ALAZANDER
          Highly unlikely.

Pudgey faces Alazander with great curiosity.

                    PUDGEY
          Why's that?

                    ALAZANDER
          You're like him. You don't have
          anywhere else to go.

                    PUDGEY
          That goes for everyone here.

                    ALAZANDER
          When I'm proven right, I think
          you'll be very impressed with me.

                    PUDGEY
          You flatter yourself.

                    ALAZANDER
          Trust me. You will always have a
          place here.
                    (beat)
          I'm going to talk to Pepper
          about buying a new unicycle.

Pudgey rolls her eyes and walks away. As she does:

                    PUDGEY
          I get no joy watching you and Tubby
          fight over me. It's immature.

EXT. PEPPER'S TRAILER - NIGHT

Tubby waddles by Pepper's trailer. Pepper is outside
picking up some trash.

                    TUBBY
          Hey Pepper, how are ticket sales?

Pepper slowly shakes his head.

                    PEPPER
          I'm sorry, but I don't think the
          posters are working.
                    (beat)
          We only have about three weeks
          left.

56.

INT. TUBBY'S TRAILER - NIGHT

COINS fall out of a piggy bank, an old-fashioned ceramic pig
statue with a slot on top for coins.

Tubby sifts through the coins.

                    TUBBY
          Seventeen dollars and twenty-three
          cents.

Tubby reclines in disappointment.

                    TUBBY
          How are we ever going to get the
          money...

Tubby picks up a piece of bacon and takes a bite.

He becomes aware of the piggy bank and faces it the other
direction.

                    TUBBY
          Don't look.

EXT. SUBURBAN STREETS - DAY

Tubby hangs another poster on a telephone pole.

He takes a break, wipes his forehead. He glances across the
street to a storefront. In the window, a sign that reads
HELP WANTED.

A lightbulb goes off in Tubby's head.

INT. PUBLIC RESTROOM - DAY (MONTAGE)

Tubby enters a restroom carrying a mop and bucket. He
attempts to clean the inside of a bathroom stall, but cannot
fit through the narrow door.

He tries his best extend his arm inside the stall and mop,
but he drops the mop and then cannot pick it up.

INT. ICE CREAM SHOP, BACK OFFICE - DAY (MONTAGE)

The owners of an ice cream shop are pouring over papers and
arguing; there is something wrong with the numbers. One of
the owners throws up his hands and walks out of the office.

The owner's eyes widen as he sees Tubby, working behind the
counter, with evidence of ice cream on his face and a
scooper in his hand.

The owner promptly points to the door.

INT. WEDDING VENUE - NIGHT (MONTAGE)

Tubby has a DSLR camera around his neck. The BRIDE and
GROOM are dancing on the dance floor.

Tubby is taking pictures of the cake.

The BEST MAN comes over and grabs Tubby's arm to direct him
to the dance floor. Tubby complies, but quickly uses his
finger to steal a bit of frosting off the cake.

INT. PIZZA PARLOR - DAY (MONTAGE)

Tubby prepares a pizza and snacks on the raw pizza dough at
the same time.

The pizza parlor owner is horrified. He hands Tubby a pizza
box and points to the door.

EXT. PIZZA PARLOR - DAY (MONTAGE)

Tubby tries to squeeze his body into the driver's seat of
the delivery car. He simply cannot fit. He tries holding
in his stomach, but can't get around the steering wheel.

He tries a running start, but doesn't fit and bounces off
the car!

EXT. SUBURBAN STREETS - DAY

Tubby leans against a telephone pole, eating a burrito.
Raoul leans on his parked cab.

                    RAOUL
          Nothing is working out?

                    TUBBY
          I'd say... none of these jobs
          really utilize my talents.

Raoul looks over his shoulder, then back at Tubby.

                    RAOUL
          I heard about some work that might
          be good for you. I have a friend
          who is looking for someone to
          collect money for him.

                    TUBBY
                (incredulously)
          Who makes a money collection when
          you can spend it on burritos?

                    RAOUL
          No, no. People owe my friend
          money. And sometimes they don't
          pay. A big fellow like you could
          intimidate them.

It dawns on Tubby.

                    TUBBY
          Gangsters.

                    RAOUL
          Yeah. But it pays well.

Tubby hesitates. Then, he shoves a bite of burrito in his
mouth and angrily turns.

                    RAOUL
          Tubby, my friend, where are you
          going?
                    (beat)
          Let me give you a ride back to the
          circus!

                    TUBBY
          I'll walk!

Tubby THROWS DOWN THE BURRITO IN ANGER.

He goes to turn, hesitates, then reaches down and picks the
burrito up off the ground.

THE CAMERA SWINGS as Tubby begins to walk, revealing that we
are across the street from:

EXT. EDGE OF CIRCUS GROUNDS - DAY

Tubby stares at the RUN-DOWN CIRCUS.

It's a heavy decision to make.

INT. DELI - DAY (MONTAGE)

Tubby enters, knocking down a display case of baked goods.
He starts waving his hands at the storeowner.

INT. LAUNDROMAT - DAY (MONTAGE)

Tubby yells at the man who attends the counter.

INT. RESTAURANT - DAY (MONTAGE)

Tubby takes a seat. The other patrons glare at him suspiciously.

INT. BIKE SHOP - DAY (MONTAGE)

Tubby argues with the proprietor of a the shop.

INT. DELI - DAY (MONTAGE)

The deli owners shakes his head "no." Tubby sprays him with water from his flower lapel.

INT. LAUNDROMAT - DAY (MONTAGE)

To the man's protest, Tubby stuffs a giant red shoes into a washing machine.

INT. RESTAURANT - DAY (MONTAGE)

The waiter brings Tubby a check. On the table before him are dozens of empty plates. Tubby rips up the check.

INT. BIKE SHOP - DAY (MONTAGE)

The bike store owner hands Tubby some money.

INT. DELI - DAY (MONTAGE)

The deli owner hands Tubby some hundred-dollar bills.

Tubby grabs a few packaged goods from the toppled display stand and exits.

INT. LAUNDROMAT - DAY (MONTAGE)

The man hands Tubby an envelop.

INT. RESTAURANT - DAY (MONTAGE)

Tubby re-enters the restaurant with the tiger on a leash. The patrons of the restaurant clear out.

Moments later, the owner is counting out dollar bills. He hands them to Tubby as the tiger licks plates clean.

60.

INT. BIKE SHOP - DAY (MONTAGE)

Tubby is leaving when something catches his eye: A VINTAGE
UNICYCLE. He grabs it and walks out of the store with it.

INT. TUBBY'S TRAILER - NIGHT

Tubby counts the money. Behind him, the unicycle rests
against a wall.

Tears cause his face make-up to run.

INT. PEPPER'S TRAILER - NIGHT

A WAD OF CASH drops in front of Pepper, who is seated at
a table eating cereal. Pepper looks up to see Tubby
grinning.

Pepper unrolls the money and counts it.

                    PEPPER
          Where did you get this?

                    TUBBY
          I earned it. To help you keep the
          circus running.

                    PEPPER
          How?

                    TUBBY
          Oh, don't worry about it. I'll do
          what I can to get us extra money.

Pepper recounts the money.

                    TUBBY
          I know it's not nearly enough, but
          we have another two weeks.

                    PEPPER
          Tubby, thank you.

Tubby nods and, after much difficulty getting through the
doorway, exits.

Pepper's television catches his attention: the news program
cuts to Yolanda Scarlet.

                    SCARLET (ON TV)
          That's right, Andy. Reports say
          that an obese man brought a tiger
          into the restaurant on Main Street
          as part of a scare tactic.

The report cuts to footage of the restaurant owner.

                    RESTAURANT OWNER (ON TV)
          It was a shake down. By a big man
          with a pet tiger. Scared all my
          customers.

The restaurant owner holds up a plate.

                    RESTAURANT OWNER (ON TV)
          At least the tiger did some
          dishwashing!

Cuts back to Scarlet.

                    SCARLET (ON TV)
          One can only speculate that this is
          the doing of mob boss, Big Lou, but
          at present there is no evidence to
          connect him to the incident. As of
          now, it seems like the mayor is not
          making good on his promise to stop
          organized crime. Back to you,
          Andy.

EXT. PUDGEY'S TRAILER - NIGHT

Tubby knocks on the door. Pudgey answers.

                    PUDGEY
          Hi ya.

                    TUBBY
          I have a surprise for you.

Pudgey smiles.

                    PUDGEY
          And what midnight snack have you
          brought tonight?

                    TUBBY
          You can't eat this surprise!

                    PUDGEY
          Tubby, I'm not sure I've ever seen
          you so excited about something you
          can't eat.

Tubby takes a step back and gestures to his side. Pudgey
sees a lump with a blanket over it.

She walks over and pulls the blanket off to reveal a NEW
UNICYCLE!

                    PUDGEY
          Oh my! Tubby! A new unicycle!

She hugs Tubby and then turns back to inspect the unicycle.

                    PUDGEY
          It's beautiful.

                    TUBBY
          Come on, let's try it out.

INT. CIRCUS TENT - NIGHT

The tent is eerily empty, except for Pudgey and Tubby.
Pudgey rides the unicycle, balancing it on a high-wire near
the ceiling of the tent. Tubby is below, looking up at her.

                    TUBBY
          It's going to be great to have you
          back in the show!

                    PUDGEY
          I feel a little shaky on it...

                    TUBBY
          If Alazander gets to add
          laser-lights and strippers, I'll
          make sure Pepper puts you back in.

                    PUDGEY
          Do you think that stripper is
          pretty?

                    TUBBY
          Umm --

Pudgey looks down at Tubby in disbelief.

                    PUDGEY
          Really?

                    TUBBY
          Pay attention!

She tips over, falling off of the high-wire. Luckily, both
she and the bike fall into a safety net suspended below.

Tubby climbs into the safety net and lies beside her.

                    TUBBY
          Okay, so you're a little rusty.

She playfully hits him.

In the darkness of stands, Alazander watches the two chat in the safety net.

Then the safety net breaks and they fall three feet to the floor.

Alazander shakes his head and disappears into the shadows.

INT. MAYOR'S OFFICE - NIGHT

Bryan and Sheriff Bob meet after hours. Sheriff Bob holds a tablet computer.

                    BRYAN
          Play it again.

On the tablet, footage of Tubby in the restaurant plays. It is grainy and low resolution.

                    BRYAN
          You can't tell that's the fat
          clown?

                    SHERIFF BOB
          I don't see a red nose or big
          shoes.

                    BRYAN
          He's obese. What more evidence do
          you need?

                    SHERIFF BOB
          He is a large man.

                    BRYAN
          See. Case closed.

                    SHERIFF BOB
          Would you like me to round up every
          fat person in the town?

On the tablet, the tiger comes into frame.

                    BRYAN
          And the tiger? How many people
          have a pet tiger?

                    SHERIFF BOB
          Maybe he's a vegan vigilante.

Bryan takes a deep breath and adapts a quieter, fatherly tone.

                    BRYAN
          Okay, I'm starting to think you're
          not taking this seriously.

Sheriff Bob looks at him in disbelief, then:

                    SHERIFF BOB
          Look, Big Lou ordered a lackey to
          shake down the owner. We should do
          nothing and use this to build a
          case against Big Lou. Forget the
          damn clown.

Bryan paces the room.

                    BRYAN
          Visit the circus grounds.

                    SHERIFF BOB
          You do realize that the press is
          starting to criticize you. You've
          done nothing to stop organized
          crime.

                    BRYAN
          I said, go to the circus grounds.

Sheriff Bob rolls his eyes.

                    SHERIFF BOB
          Why would I do that?

                    BRYAN
          To see if the fat clown has an
          excuse for where he's been.

INT. TUBBY'S TRAILER - NIGHT

Kimmy sets up her laptop. Tubby eats a candy bar.

                    TUBBY
          Where have you been?

                    KIMMY
          Dad grounded me for helping you not
          get arrested.

                    TUBBY
          That seems harsh.

Kimmy steps back; the laptop is positioned just right.

                    KIMMY
          Take a look. This is episode one
          of our web series, Chasing Tubby.

ON THE LAPTOP: creepy music starts to play. A narrator with
a deep, dramatic voice speaks over black-and-white footage
of the town.

                    NARRATOR
          On tonight's episode of Chasing
          Tubby, a team of school children
          are determined to track down a fat
          clown by the name of Tubby.

A blurry black-and-white photo of Tubby appears on the
screen.

                    NARRATOR
          But is Tubby man or myth?

Grainy, blurry old photos of a backyard birthday party
appear on screen.

                    NARRATOR
          Since second grade, stories were
          told of a Fat Clown stealing
          birthday cakes at parties. This
          has lead to drastic measures by the
          people of Chiffon Ridge.

Cut to talking-head footage of Jacob's mom.

                    JACOB'S MOM
          We had to buy two birthday cakes.
          It's just what we have to do during
          this crazy time. It's a way of
          life.

Cut to green night-vision footage of a forest.

                    NARRATOR
          Neighborhood kids have gone in
          search of the Fat Clown.

There is a noise in the forest.

                    GINGER
          What was that noise? Did you hear
          it?

                    JACOB
          It sounded like honking...

                    NARRATOR
          But the search often came with dire
          consequences.

Cut to talking-head footage of a silhouetted person,
obscured to protect his identity.

                ANONYMOUS PERSON
          I grounded my son for three weeks.

Cut to footage from Jacob's birthday party.

                    NARRATOR
          Today, neighborhood kids will try
          to lure the fat clown to them.

Kimmy appears on camera standing beside the birthday cake.

                KIMMY (ON-SCREEN)
          Butter-cream frosting. This should
          do the trick.

Cut to talking-head of Jacob's mom.

                  JACOB'S MOM
          I'll admit, I'm unsure about how
          this is going to pan out.

Cut to a poorly-made graphic title card that reads "Chasing
Tubby"

BACK IN THE ROOM: Kimmy turns to Tubby with a grin.

                    KIMMY
          It's awesome, ain't it?

Tubby shoves a handful of popcorn into his mouth.

                    TUBBY
          Delicious!

ON THE LAPTOP: the smartphone footage of Tubby breaking into
Jacob's backyard and stealing the cake plays.

IN THE ROOM, Tubby salivates.

                    TUBBY
          That was a good cake.

Kimmy jumps up and stops the video. She turns to Tubby.

                    KIMMY
          Here's the plan. This video is
          already online. Everyone at school
          is passing it around. It's going
          viral. Ginger's been tweeting it
          like there's no tomorrow. Next, we
          hold a fundraiser called "Meet the
          Circus Folk." People can come
          wander the grounds, meet the
          performers, see the animals, play
          on a trampoline, and most of all,
          they get to meet the legendary
          Tubby the Fat Clown.

                    TUBBY
          It's ingenious. I'll run it by
          Pepper.

KNOCK! KNOCK!

Tubby and Kimmy exchange worried glances. Tubby waddles
over and answers the door. It's Sheriff Bob and two police
officers.

                    SHERIFF BOB
          You. Are you the fat clown who --

Sheriff Bob spots Kimmy.

                    SHERIFF BOB
          What are <u>you</u> doing here?

                    KIMMY
          Tubby is my friend.

Sheriff Bob looks at Kimmy suspiciously, then turns back to
Tubby.

                    SHERIFF BOB
          Can you tell us your whereabouts
          this afternoon?

                    KIMMY
          He was here. With me. We were
          working on a video project.

                    SHERIFF BOB
          What sort of video project?

                    KIMMY
          It's for a website.

68.

                    SHERIFF BOB
          A web video... with an older clown
          and an underaged girl.

Sheriff Bob and the other officers exchanged worried
glances.

                    TUBBY
          No, no. It's not like that. You
          want to see?

INT. TUBBY'S TRAILER - MOMENTS LATER

Sheriff Bob and the officers have finished watching the
video.

                    SHERIFF BOB
          Oh, your father's not going to like
          this.

                    KIMMY
          Why? We didn't break any rules, did
          we?

Sheriff Bob shakes his head.

                    OFFICER #1
                 (excitedly)
          Hey, can we watch it again?

EXT. SCHOOLYARD - DAY

Kimmy hands a boy a ticket in exchange for some cash.

                    KIMMY
          Awesome! I'll see you at the
          fundraiser.

Kimmy turns to find a group of kids with money in their
hands. She starts selling tickets to them.

                    KIMMY
          C'mon, get them before they're all
          sold out!

The history teacher approaches Kimmy.

                    HISTORY TEACHER
          Young lady, you're not supposed to
          be selling things on school
          property.

                    KIMMY
          They're tickets to a fundraiser at
          the circus! You can come hang out
          with the circus people for a day.

                    HISTORY TEACHER
          I see.

The history teacher looks around for other teachers, then
turns back to Kimmy.

                    HISTORY TEACHER
          I'll take one.

EXT. CIRCUS GROUNDS - DAY

Under Pepper's direction, a banner is raised that reads
"Meet the Circus Folk."

                    PEPPER
          That's perfect, hold it there!

Alazander approaches.

                    ALAZANDER
          This just delays the inevitable.

                    PEPPER
          Maybe. Maybe not.

Pepper walks the grounds, surveying the preparations. Velvet
ropes have been brought in to make queues. A catering truck
unloads some tables. Performers pick up trash.

                    PEPPER
          Well, if we bring in enough money
          tomorrow, we can pay off the bank!
               (beat)
          Or, at least maybe Tubby can stop
          working a second job.

Alazander's curiosity is piqued.

                    ALAZANDER
          A second job?

                    PEPPER
          Yeah, he's been doing odds-and-ends
          to bring in some extra money,
          apparently.

                    ALAZANDER
          Is that so?

INT. DRY CLEANERS - DAY

The woman behind the counter quivers and reaches below the
counter. She pulls out an envelope and hands it to Tubby.
Tubby peaks inside and nods.

                    OLD WOMAN
          Son, don't you ever think about
          what you're doing?

Tubby is caught off-guard by the question.

                    TUBBY
          Well, usually, I'm thinking about
          danish.

                    OLD WOMAN
          Is this what you want to be doing?

Tubby goes to answer, but then is at a loss for words. He
turns and approaches the exit.

                    TUBBY
          I'd rather be eating danish.

INT. HARDWARE STORE - DAY

ROLAND -- 80's, tired, frail -- shakes his head at Tubby.

                    ROLAND
          No! I am done with this. Not
          another penny! Not another penny!

                    TUBBY
          How about a nickel? Like a couple
          hundred of them?

                    ROLAND
          You are dense.

                    TUBBY
          Oh, fine bring my weight into this.

                    ROLAND
          I'm _not_ paying.

                    TUBBY
          Look, I don't think the people I
          work for will go for that.

The old man squints at Tubby, as if peering deep into his
soul.

                    ROLAND
          You're not like most of them.

                    TUBBY
          Again with my weight. Look --

                    ROLAND
          No, I mean you. Your personality.

                    TUBBY
          Oh.

                    ROLAND
          Why are you helping them?

                    TUBBY
          I don't want to be. But I have my
          reasons.

                    ROLAND
          Are those reasons worth becoming
          one of them? A criminal? Someone
          we teach our children to be scared
          of?

                    TUBBY
          Hey, I like children!

                    ROLAND
          And what would children say if they
          knew what sort of business you were
          into?

Tubby looks disappointed.

EXT. PARK - DAY

Tubby meets with Frank Slapnuts on a bench. Tubby hands him
the envelope.

                    TUBBY
          From the dry cleaners. Roland's
          Hardware Store refuses to pay.

                    FRANK SLAPNUTS
          Is that so?

                    TUBBY
          Yes.

Frank Slapnuts nods.

                         FRANK SLAPNUTS
                    Okay. I'll deal with the old man
                    later.

Frank Slapnuts reaches inside the envelope, takes out a
handful of hundred dollar bills and hands them to Tubby.

                         FRANK SLAPNUTS
                    Next week, let's meet at the
                    pizzeria on First Street.

Frank walks off.

Tubby flips through the dollar bills unenthusiastically.

INT. CUPCAKE HOUSE - NIGHT

Rows and rows of cupcakes lay on the counter. Miss Rolly
breathes in the smell. Tubby salivates.

                         MISS ROLLY
                    They smell delicious, don't they?

                         TUBBY
                         (unenthusiastically)
                    Yeah, they do.

                         MISS ROLLY
                    Uh-oh. What's wrong now?

                         TUBBY
                    Nothing a cupcake can't solve!

Tubby reaches for one, but Miss Rolly hits his hand with a
rolling pin.

                         MISS ROLLY
                    No. These are for your fundraiser
                    tomorrow!

SIRENS blare from outside.

                         MISS ROLLY
                    What in the hell is that racket?

EXT. CUPCAKE HOUSE - NIGHT

Miss Rolly, Tubby, and some patrons exit the Cupcake House.
Down the block, a building is engulfed in flames.
Firefighters pile out of a fire engine.

                    MISS ROLLY
          That's old man Roland's hardware
          store! He's had that place for
          fifty years.

Tubby is horrified by the sight.

                    MISS ROLLY
          Despicable. If I knew who did that
          to old man Roland, I'd beat him
          like an egg.

Tubby lowers his head. A tear rolls down his cheek.

EXT. CIRCUS GROUNDS - DAY

The fundraiser is packed.

AT THE ENTRANCE, Pepper is dressed in full ringmaster
apparel welcoming people to the circus grounds.

                    PEPPER
          Welcome! Welcome to Pepper's
          Groove-tastic Circus!

IN A BOOTH, Kimmy stands before a large TV mounted on a
platform. It plays the episode of "Chasing Tubby." Jacob
stands beside her, totally smitten. Ginger plays with her
phone.

                    KIMMY
          Come one. Come all. This is the
          home of the legendary Tubby the Fat
          Clown!

Jacob smiles at Kimmy.

                    JACOB
          This is so cool.

                    KIMMY
          Yeah, it is.

UNDER A TENT, Miss Rolly sells cupcakes. She turns to her
assistant, JULIENNE.

                    MISS ROLLY
          Call the kitchen, tell them to
          start baking more pronto!

                    JULIENNE
          Yes ma'am.

Pudgey eats one of the cupcakes.

74.

                    PUDGEY
          Miss Rolly, we sure do miss your
          cooking around here.

                    MISS ROLLY
          Oh, I loved cooking for y'all, but
          it was time to move on.
               (beat)
          Business is booming at the shop.
          And by the looks of it, you guys
          might be busy again too!

                    PUDGEY
          Tubby has put a lot of work into
          this fundraiser. I hope it does
          work. Otherwise...

She doesn't complete her sentence.

                    MISS ROLLY
          If things don't work out, I could
          use some extra hands. How good is
          your baking?

                    PUDGEY
          Don't know. Tubby eats the
          ingredients before they make it to
          the oven.

IN FRONT OF ANOTHER TENT, a line of people are queued up. A
banner reads "Can You Eat Like Tubby?"

                    CIRCUS HAND
          If you can eat this cake faster
          than Tubby, you win a special
          prize!

                    PATRON
          Bring it on.

                    CIRCUS HAND
          Ready, set, eat!

They gorge on cake. Tubby finishes his cake. The patron
still has half of a cake left!

                    CIRCUS HAND
          Tubby wins!

BACK AT THE ENTRANCE, the history teacher approaches Pepper.

                    HISTORY TEACHER
          So, are you hiring?

ELSEWHERE, Zelda has a snake resting on her shoulders.
Visitors watch nervously as she dances with it. Jacob
stares at her with his jaw dropped. He is frozen.

                    ZELDA
          Honey, are you okay?

BACK AT THE ENTRANCE, Alazander wanders over to Pepper.

                    PEPPER
          We are doing fantastic! We are
          even pre-selling tickets to future
          shows. Can you imagine that?
          Selling tickets to shows in the
          future!

                    ALAZANDER
          Delightful.

                    PEPPER
          I can't wait to hand the bank a
          check and be done with them.

Pepper points in the direction of some press. Among them is
Yolanda Scarlet, getting ready to go on air.

                    PEPPER
          Look! Reporters! With this
          momentum, maybe I can finally put
          on the show of a lifetime!

Yolanda Scarlet approaches Alazander and Pepper.

                    SCARLET
          Alazander, how's my favorite
          magician?

                    ALAZANDER
          Uninspired by this... silliness.

                    SCARLET
          Tell me, do you possess the magic
          in you? Or is it all in your wand?

Alazander is surprised by the question.

                    ALAZANDER
          In my wand, of course.

                    SCARLET
          May I try some magic?

                    ALAZANDER
          I doubt you want to play with my
          wand on television, Miss Scarlet.

Alazander grins and walks off.

INT. MAYOR'S OFFICE - DAY

Bryan and Sheriff Bob watch a news report by Yolanda
Scarlet.

                    SCARLET (ON TV)
          The fundraiser at Pepper's Circus
          is the place to be this Saturday
          morning. Locals and tourists alike
          are pouring in to meet the circus
          folk.

                    BRYAN
          Who issued these people a permit?

                    SHERIFF BOB
          It's on private property. They
          don't need a permit.

                    BRYAN
          Why is every law in this town
          ass-backwards?

News footage shows Kimmy posing and smiling with a lot of
the circus folk.

                    SCARLET (ON TV)
          Even the mayor's daughter is having
          a great time. She's the brainchild
          behind "Chasing Tubby," a popular
          web series that has helped to stir
          interest.

                    KIMMY (ON TV)
          The circus is awesome! It's
          amazing. And I think everyone
          should watch the web series and
          then come see the circus in action!
          Clowns, magic --

Jacob jumps into frame.

                    JACOB (ON TV)
          There's even this naked woman --

Kimmy pushes Jacob out of frame.

INT. CIRCUS TENT, BACKSTAGE - NIGHT

The fundraiser is over. Everyone is gathered inside of the
circus tent.

                    PEPPER
          Great job, everyone! And a special
          thanks to Tubby and his friend
          Kimmy, who thought up this
          brilliant plan!

The circus performers cheer. Kimmy smiles broadly.

                    PEPPER
          Not only are people excited about
          the circus, but I can finally pay
          off our bank loans!

More cheers.

                    PEPPER
          Let's celebrate!

POP! A bottle of champagne is opened. Music starts up.
People start dancing.

Pepper finds his way to Kimmy and Tubby.

                    PEPPER
          I cannot thank the two of you
          enough. From the bottom of my
          heart, thank you.

                    TUBBY
          It was mostly Kimmy's doing.

                    PEPPER
          Are you old enough to have a job?
          We might need to bring you on
          board!

Alazander sidles up alongside them.

                    ALAZANDER
          I'm sure the girl's father would be
          very interested to know where she
          is.

                         PEPPER
               Really? She saved the circus and
               you're going to rat her out?

Alazander says nothing.

                         PEPPER
               Well, that really takes the cake.

Tubby's eyes light up.

                         TUBBY
               There's cake?

Pudgey comes up behind Tubby and places her hands on his
shoulders.

                         PUDGEY
               Tubby, dance with me!

Tubby and Pudgey walk off. They start dancing awkwardly.

Pepper watches them, beaming. He turns to where Alazander
was standing, but finds he has gone.

EXT. CIRCUS TENT - NIGHT

The sound of revelry comes from within the tent. Alazander
stands outside, alone and shaking his head.

Pepper emerges from the tent.

                         PEPPER
               Is something troubling you?

Alazander walks further from the tent.

                         PEPPER
               Don't ignore me, Alazander. I
               thought you wanted to save the
               circus!

Alazander turns to face Pepper.

                         ALAZANDER
               I did.

It dawns on Pepper.

                         PEPPER
               You just wanted to be the one to do
               it. You're jealous someone pulled
               off this magic trick before you.

Alazander says nothing.

> PEPPER
> We're all in this together. Who
> are you trying to fool?

Alazander glances in the direction of the tent. Through a
plastic window, Tubby and Pudgey continue the awkward dance
of two fat people.

> PEPPER
> Did you really think you'd win her
> over by being the savior of the
> circus?

> ALAZANDER
> It was a logical plan.

> PEPPER
> Tubby is not going anywhere. You
> had better get over this.

> ALAZANDER
> I still have one trick left up my
> sleeve.

EXT. CIRCUS GROUNDS - DAY (NEWS BROADCAST)

Yolanda Scarlet reports from in front of the circus tent.

> SCARLET
> Breaking news. Pepper's Circus,
> the darling of the town and media
> last week with its fundraiser and
> outreach program, has been hit with
> scandal.

The broadcast cuts to grainy footage from a security
camera: the tiger enters the stands, approaches Kimmy and
her friends.

> SCARLET
> An anonymous source leaked this
> footage which shows what appears to
> be a tiger entering the bleachers
> and threatening to attack children.

Cut back to Scarlet.

> SCARLET
> Luckily, circus performers were
> able to stop the animal, but this
> tape raises serious questions about
> the safety of the circus.

INT. MAYOR'S OFFICE - DAY

Bryan and Sheriff Bob watch the broadcast.

                    BRYAN
          Whoa, whoa, whoa. Is that Kimmy?

                    SHERIFF BOB
          Hard to say. The footage is
          grainy --

                    BRYAN
          It is!

Sheriff Bob rolls his eyes.

                    BRYAN
          Finally, the opportunity we have
          been waiting for!

                    SHERIFF BOB
          You know, there's a web series.
          This could staged for --

                    BRYAN
          Shut the circus down! Do not worry
          about the legality of it. People
          won't ask questions when I act in
          defense of my little girl!

Sheriff Bob laughs.

                    SHERIFF BOB
          This has nothing to do with your
          daughter.

                    BRYAN
          I'm working up some tears.

                    SHERIFF BOB
          I've had enough of this tomfoolery.

                    BRYAN
          I'll just need an onion or
          something before the press
          conference.

                    SHERIFF BOB
          Okay. I'm done.

                    BRYAN
          Excuse me?

Sheriff Bob rips his badge off his jacket and hurls it at
Bryan.

                    SHERIFF BOB
          Do what you'd like. I'm done.

Sheriff Bob storms out.

                    BRYAN
          You can't quit!

                    SHERIFF BOB
          Yes, I can.

He exits, leaving Bryan standing alone.

EXT. CIRCUS TENT - DAY

A foreboding sign is taped to the door of the circus tent.
It reads: "Closed by Order of the Police. Signed, Deputy
Mayor Jack Lloyd."

Tubby, Pudgey, and a group of other circus performers stare
at it, bewildered.

Alazander approaches the group.

                    ALAZANDER
          What a pity. Surely, Pepper will
          need to step down after this
          embarrassment.

Tubby faces him. There is rage in his eyes.

                    TUBBY
          You gave Scarlet that tape!

                    ALAZANDER
          That's a harsh accusation.

Tubby storms off. Pudgey turns to Alazander. There are
tears in her eyes that say "how could you?"

INT. MAYOR'S OFFICE - DAY

Bryan sits across from Pepper. Mr. Mudword is also present,
pacing off to the side of the room.

82.

                    PEPPER
          You have no justification for
          closing the circus!

                    BRYAN
          My daughter was almost killed. How
          do you want me to react?

                    PEPPER
          Your daughter is our biggest fan
          and fundraiser.

Bryan cringes at this.

                    BRYAN
          Here's what we're going to do. Mr.
          Mudword here has agreed to buy the
          circus and, more importantly, the
          land it sits on.

                    MUDWORD
          I am prepared to pay handsomely.

                    PEPPER
          I'm not interested.

Mudword and Bryan laugh.

                    BRYAN
          You see, Mr. Mudword is an
          accomplished real estate developer.
          He will put a high rise on the land
          and --

                    PEPPER
          No.

Pepper stands up.

                    PEPPER
          I said, I'm not selling.

                    BRYAN
          Be reasonable.

                    PEPPER
          I'll bring this to the courts if I
          have to. You had no reason to shut
          us down. We'll fight it.

Bryan also stands.

                    BRYAN
          And if I suddenly feel very
          concerned for my little girl's
          safety?

                    PEPPER
          Good luck trying to get her to
          testify. Good day, gentlemen.

Pepper turns on a heel and exits. The door slams behind
him.

Mudword addresses Bryan.

                    MUDWORD
          If you cannot exert the pull
          required, there are other
          influential forces in this town.

Bryan shakes his hands at this statement.

                    BRYAN
          Now, I know you're not referring to
          the gangsters --

                    MUDWORD
          I merely question whether this is
          the most powerful office in the
          town.

Mudword smiles and exits.

INT. KIMMY'S HOUSE, KIMMY'S BEDROOM - NIGHT

Kimmy edits a new video on his laptop when Bryan barges into
the room.

                    BRYAN
          I've scheduled a press conference
          tomorrow. You're going to tell
          everyone how you were terrified by
          the tiger. You will say that the
          circus folk scared you into helping
          them raise money and undermine me.

                    KIMMY
          No I'm not.

                    BRYAN
          Uh, yes, you will.

84.

                    KIMMY
          Why are you being so mean to them?

                    BRYAN
          Mean? I'm trying to make those
          criminals disappear! To keep law
          and order in this town!

                    KIMMY
          I won't do it.

                    BRYAN
          You will.

                    KIMMY
          They're not bad guys!

                    BRYAN
          Don't talk back to me.

                    KIMMY
          You've made all these big promises
          about the gangsters. How you were
          going to round them up and put them
          in jail. You've done nothing, Dad.
          Instead you pick on some poor
          clown. You're pathetic!

Bryan is fuming. He goes to say something, but then just
leaves and slams the door.

Tears flood Kimmy's eyes. She eyes the window.

                    KIMMY
          I've got to warn Tubby.

INT. PIZZA PARLOR - NIGHT

Tubby sits across from Frankie Slapnuts. He pops garlic
knots into his mouth as though they were M&Ms.

                    TUBBY
          The police closed the circus.

                    FRANK SLAPNUTS
          So, you need more work?

                    TUBBY
          No. I'm done. I was just doing
          this to get some extra money to
          help the circus.

Frankie shakes his head.

                    FRANK SLAPNUTS
          No, no. You work for us.

                    TUBBY
          I don't need the money anymore.

                    FRANK SLAPNUTS
          How do I know you won't rat us out?

                    TUBBY
          I would never.

                    FRANK SLAPNUTS
          The mayor isn't too happy with us
          gangsters.

                    TUBBY
          He's not too fond of us circus
          folk either.

                    FRANK SLAPNUTS
          We can't let you go that easily.
          The mayor. He's determined to take
          a bite out of crime.

Tubby leans forward, intrigued.

                    TUBBY
          Crime? Is that some new European
          dessert?

                    FRANK SLAPNUTS
          What?

                    TUBBY
          Look, I won't say a word.

Frankie opens his jacket slightly, revealing a concealed
pistol.

                    FRANK SLAPNUTS
          I'll decided when you're done
          working for us.

Frankie closes his jacket. Tubby lowers his head. Frankie
hands an envelop to Tubby.

                    FRANK SLAPNUTS
          You've been promoted to
          kidnappings.

Tubby removes a photo from the envelop: A PHOTO OF PEPPER!
Tubby's fat jaw drops.

Frankie sips some espresso.

>   FRANK SLAPNUTS
>   I don't know who this guy is, but
>   Big Lou says to bring him to the
>   docks tonight. Pier 73. Alive.

>   TUBBY
>   I won't do it.

Tubby stands and Frankie follows. Another two men in the
pizzeria also rise. Tubby is blocked.

>   FRANK SLAPNUTS
>   Sit down.

Tubby spots the kitchen door. He makes a break for it.

INT. PIZZA PARLOR, KITCHEN - NIGHT

Tubby rushes through the kitchen. He grabs a small cheese
pie as he goes. He tips over a cart of dough to block the
way. Frankie and the other gangsters trip over it!

Tubby grabs a can of garlic powder, rips off the top, and
shucks it forward. GARLIC POWDER CLOUDS THE KITCHEN!

EXT. STREETS - NIGHT

Tubby bursts into an alley way behind the pizza parlor. He
runs down the alley way, eating the pizza as he goes.

He turns into the street and HONKS his nose.

RAOUL'S CAB APPEARS.

INT. TAXI CAB - NIGHT

Tubby tries to squeeze in the backseat. He is forced to
drop the half pizza he has not eaten.

>   TUBBY
>   Go! Go!

TIRES SQUEAL! The cab pulls away with Tubby's body
half-hanging out the door.

EXT. STREETS - NIGHT

BANG! BANG! Frankie Slapnuts FIRES at the cab as it
disappears down the road!

The cab is soon gone.

Frankie gazes at the half-eaten pizza lying on the asphalt.

EXT. SUBURBAN STREETS - MOMENTS LATER

The taxi cab rolls along. Tubby's body still hangs out of
the cab. The cab stops and causes Tubby to tumble out
onto the street.

Raoul rolls down the window.

                    RAOUL
          What did you do?

                    TUBBY
          Me?!

                    RAOUL
          I get you a job! And then they try
          to shoot you?!

Tubby looks at the back tire. It is flat and riddled with
holes. There are several gunshot holes in the back of the
car.

                    TUBBY
          I hope you have good insurance.

                    RAOUL
          I don't think my policy covers
          gangster damage.

Raoul rushes out of the car to take a look. He mutters some
vulgarities under his breath.

                    TUBBY
          Take me back to the circus.

                    RAOUL
          I call a mechanic first. To fix
          tire.

                    TUBBY
          Can't you drive me back first?

                    RAOUL
          And ruin the wheel? No way.

                    TUBBY
          Don't you have a spare tire?

                    RAOUL
          The only spare tire is around your
          waist.

                    TUBBY
          Ouch.

                    RAOUL
          I cannot drive you. You need to
          walk.

Tubby is horrified.

                    TUBBY
          Walk? It's a mile from here.

Raoul pats Tubby's stomach.

                    RAOUL
          I think you've got enough fuel for
          the journey.

TIRES SCREECHING. Down the road, a mob car goes speeding
around a corner. But it does not head for Tubby and Raoul.

                    TUBBY
          They are heading for the circus!

Tubby breaks out into a run (as close to a run as he can
muster).

INT. CUPCAKE HOUSE - NIGHT

Miss Rolly is wiping down the counter when something catches
her eye. She looks up to see A GANGSTER CAR BARRELING DOWN
THE STREET.

She returns to wiping the counter. The oven DINGS. She
tosses the rag over her shoulder and pulls a tray out of the
oven.

Something else catches her eye. She looks up to see TUBBY
RUNNING DOWN THE STREET.

                    MISS ROLLY
          Oh, hell. Julienne, cover for me,
          will you?

Miss Rolly grabs her rolling pin and exits.

EXT. CIRCUS GROUNDS - NIGHT

Tubby arrives at the circus grounds, just as a mob car
speeds away.

                    TUBBY
          Oh no!

INT. PEPPER'S TRAILER - NIGHT

Tubby enters Pepper's trailer. The place is a mess. The
walls are riddled with bullet holes.

Pudgey and Alazander are already inside. Pudgey is treating
a gunshot wound in Alazander's arm.

                    PUDGEY
          They took Pepper!

Tubby glares at Alazander.

                    TUBBY
          You must be pretty happy about
          that.

                    ALAZANDER
          I admit, things have gotten a bit
          out of control.

                    TUBBY
          You ordered a hit on Pepper?!

                    ALAZANDER
          Don't be ridiculous.

                    TUBBY
          He didn't go away after you gave
          Scarlet that security footage, so
          you try to have him killed?

                    ALAZADER
          I did not order a hit.

                    TUBBY
          Why don't you put yourself in a box
          and let me saw you half?

                    ALAZANDER
          Oh, go eat a sandwich.

Pudgey is in tears.

                    PUDGEY
          Boys, focus! They're going to
          torture Pepper and make him sell
          the circus.

                    TUBBY
          We have to go after him.

                    ALAZANDER
          That would require knowing
          where they took him.

Tubby takes a deep breath. He hesitates.

                    TUBBY
          The gangster's hideout is on Pier
          73.

Alazander and Pudgey look at him incredulously.

                    PUDGEY
          How exactly do you know such
          things?

Alazander puts it together.

                    ALAZANDER
          So, that's where you've been
          earning some side money...

Tubby swallows his pride.

                    TUBBY
          Yes, I did some work for Big Lou.
          For extra money. To help keep the
          circus afloat.

Pudgey lowers her head.

                    ALAZANDER
          You're an accomplice to kidnapping,
          then. Wait until the mayor finds
          out.

                    TUBBY
          He will never know.

                    ALAZANDER
          I guess it depends on how strong
          your relationship with that girl
          is.

Tubby is confused, then turns to find KIMMY STANDING IN THE
DOORWAY of the trailer. Kimmy is in shock.

                    TUBBY
          Kimmy, I did what I had to. I --

                    KIMMY
          My dad was right. You are bad
          people.

Kimmy steps back slowly, as if she feels she is in danger.
Tubby approaches slowly.

                    KIMMY
          Stay the heck away from me!

                    TUBBY
          Kimmy, listen --

Kimmy turns and runs off. Tubby chases.

Pudgey starts hysterically crying. Alazander comforts her.

EXT. CIRCUS GROUNDS - NIGHT

Tubby follows Kimmy.

                    TUBBY
          Kimmy, listen, please.

Kimmy stops, turns. Tubby heaves and catches his breath.

                    KIMMY
          My dad was right. You are a
          criminal!

                    TUBBY
          Look, I did some bad things to try
          to save the circus. And now
          things are worse because I tried to
          do a good thing. Like using
          margarine instead of regular butter
          in cookies.

Kimmy is visibly confused.

                    TUBBY (CONT'D)
          But then you came along! You and
          your web series were the secret
          ingredients. Now we have a
          fully-baked show!

                    KIMMY
          I wish I had never helped you!

There is some commotion. They turn in the direction of
Pudgey's trailer.

THE UNICYCLE COMES FLYING OUT OF THE TRAILER!

                    TUBBY
          Oh great.

Tubby rushes past Kimmy and toward the trailer. He picks
the unicycle up and leans it carefully against the trailer.

The door opens again and Pudgey sticks her head out of the
doorway.

                    PUDGEY
          Go away!

                    TUBBY
          I'm going to make this right.

                    PUDGEY
          How?

Tubby looks at Pudgey and then at Kimmy.

                    TUBBY
          I'm going to rescue Pepper.

EXT. DOCKS - NIGHT

The taxi cab pulls up to the docks. The docks are eerie and
seemingly abandoned.

MIDDLE EASTERN MUSIC BLASTS, making their arrival very
obvious.

INT. TAXI CAB - NIGHT

                    TUBBY
          Turn that off!

                    RAOUL
          It is beautiful music!

                    TUBBY
          We'll wake up everyone sleeping
          with the fishes.

Raoul kills the music and comes to a stop.

Tubby looks out the window.

                    RAOUL
          Tubby, my friend, are you sure
          about this?

Tubby nervously takes a bite of a Three Muskateers bar.

                    TUBBY
          I need to steal Pepper back.

Raoul is shaken up.

                    RAOUL
          I should never have gotten you that
          job.

Raoul goes to take a sip of coffee, but Tubby grabs it! He
downs the coffee in one gulp!

                    RAOUL
          Hey!

                    TUBBY
          Just be ready to go!

INT. DOCKS, PIER 73 - NIGHT

Frankie Slapnuts punches Pepper in the face.

                    FRANK SLAPNUTS
          You will sign the document.

Pepper doesn't say anything.

                    FRANK SLAPNUTS
          Listen. My friend wants to pay you
          handsomely for your circus. Why
          don't you just say yes and he will
          write you a nice, big check.

                    PEPPER
          It's not about money. It's about
          putting on the show of a lifetime.
          I haven't done that yet.

Frankie pulls a gun and raises it to Pepper.

                    FRANK SLAPNUTS
          The show's over. It's curtains for
          you.

PEPPER IS SNATCHED! Frankie FIRES! Misses!

Tubby, carrying Pepper in the chair, runs behind a shipping
crate. He sets the chair down.

                    TUBBY
          You're heavier than a cake!

                    PEPPER
          Tubby! You fat idiot! Get me
          untied!

Tubby takes off his giant clown shoe and uses it to break
the chain holding Pepper to the chair.

Frankie and three gangsters now hover behind Tubby and
Pepper. Guns are drawn.

                    FRANK SLAPNUTS
          You're dead.

Tubby summons some courage and faces Frankie.

                    TUBBY
          Would you believe me if I said Big
          Lou has ordered me to take this man
          to him?

                    FRANK SLAPNUTS
          No.

                    TUBBY
          Do you want to take that chance?

Frank Slapnuts raises his gun to Tubby.

                    FRANK SLAPNUTS
          I've had enough of your fat face.

Tubby stares Frankie down. Frankie is about to pull the
trigger...

CRASH! RAOUL'S TAXI CAB COMES CRASHING THROUGH THE
WAREHOUSE GATE!

The gangsters are disoriented. They scramble.

                    TUBBY
          Let's go!

Tubby leads Pepper out a side door.

The gangsters scramble and RETURN FIRE at the taxi cab.
BULLETS RICOCHET OFF THE VEHICLE.

EXT. DOCKS - NIGHT

Tubby and Pepper run. Frankie and the gangsters pursue.

BANG! TIRES SQUEALING!

                    TUBBY
          I don't see Raoul!

BANG!

They take cover behind some shipping boxes. Tubby peers
over the top of the crate to see Frankie Slapnuts.

Tubby stands and fires his flower-lapel. Water hits Frankie
square in the face, causing him to stumble backwards over
the edge of the pier and into the water.

Distant YELLING and SHOUTS echo around the dock buildings.

Tubby and Pepper make a break for it, running back toward
the street.

HONK! HONK!

                    TUBBY
          Where is he?

Gangsters turn a corner and are now in rapid pursuit of
Tubby, who cannot outrun them.

Tubby and Pepper turn another corner -- ITS A DEAD END!

                    PEPPER
          Go back! Go back!

They turn, but GANGSTERS ARE CLOSING IN. They're trapped.

A FLASH OF SMOKE! Alazander has appeared. He quickly fires
his wand at some oil drums. KABOOM!

Everyone is disoriented. Machine guns are fired
aimlessly...

Tubby and Pepper run through the black smoke...

A SECOND EXPLOSION consumes an entire building and the
pursuing gangsters are stopped.

Alazander stumbles backwards and then drops to the floor.
His wand falls from his hands.

Tubby and Pepper rush to him, but they are cut off by
another explosion! Dark smoke obstructs their view.

Tubby goes to run inside of cloud of black smoke, but Pepper
grabs his arm.

> PEPPER
> Tubby, it's not safe!

Tubby glares at Pepper, torn.

> PEPPER
> They're going to go after the
> circus. We need to get to back.

Tubby HONKS his red clown nose.

HEADLIGHTS shine in Tubby's face; Raoul has returned.

Raoul sticks his head out the driver-side window.

> RAOUL
> Tubby, my friend, I don't get it.
> Where is the cake?

INT. KIMMY'S HOUSE, KIMMY'S BEDROOM - NIGHT

Kimmy climbs back in through the window. The lights are
thrown on. Bryan and Vanessa are there waiting for him.

> BRYAN
> Where have you been?

> KIMMY
> Ginger's house?

> VANESSA
> I called Ginger's mom. She says
> you weren't there.

> KIMMY
> Ok. I was at Jacob's house. He's
> sort of, eh, my boyfriend.

> BRYAN
> Do you really think we are so
> clueless? You were at the circus
> hanging out with the clown.

Kimmy lowers her head.

> BRYAN
> They are bad people.

Kimmy doesn't protest.

                    KIMMY
          You're right. The fat clown. He
          works for the gangsters.

Bryan smiles.

                    BRYAN
          You wanted to see me act on my
          word? I'm going to go down to the
          circus and beat that fat clown
          myself.

                    KIMMY
          Take me with you.

Bryan turns back, curious.

                    KIMMY
          I want to see you do it.

Vanessa is nervous. There is an awkward silence.

                    VANESSA
          Kimmy, why don't you let your
          father --

                    BRYAN
               (to Kimmy)
          Fine. If you want to watch me beat
          the crap out of that fat idiot, get
          in the car.

EXT. CIRCUS GROUNDS - NIGHT

The taxi cab arrives back at the circus grounds. Tubby
wiggles his way out of the cab. Pepper follows.

Raoul rounds down his window.

                    RAOUL
          Pretty good driving, eh, Mr. Tubby?

                    TUBBY
          The best!

                    RAOUL
          How about a tip?

Tubby hesitates. Then:

                    TUBBY
          If you got a frownie, eat a
          brownie!

98.

Raoul is confused.

Pudgey rushes toward Tubby and Pepper.

> PUDGEY
> You're safe!

Pudgey throws her arms around Pepper.

> PEPPER
> Tubby and Alazander were amazing.

Pudgey turns to Tubby.

> PUDGEY
> (surprised)
> Alazander went with you? Where is
> he?

Tubby doesn't answer and that answers Pudgey's question.

> TUBBY
> We need to gather everyone now.

INT. CIRCUS TENT - NIGHT

Tubby, Pudgey, Pepper, and all of the circus folk are
gathered in the main tent.

> PEPPER
> Any minute now, Big Lou's gangsters
> will be here to kill us all and
> destroy the circus!

Vlad shrieks.

> VLAD
> What are we going to do?

> BEARDED LADY
> We're going to fight!

Billy cracks his whip.

> BILLY
> My tigers are ready to fight!

> ROBERT
> The cannon is loaded!

There is chatter and commotion among the circus folk.

                    PEPPER
          Anyone who doesn't want to fight
          should leave now.

There are some murmurs but nobody leaves. Vlad steps
forward.

                    VLAD
          The Amazing Air Dancers will fight.
          It is what Alazander would have
          wanted.

                    TED
          Lighting will also fight. We'll
          light up their world.

The tiger roars.

                    ZELDA
          Let's give them a show to die for!

The circus folk cheer!

EXT. DOCKS - NIGHT

The police department and fire department are at the docks,
putting out the fire and reviewing the crime scene.

Yolanda Scarlet and her cameraman are there, reporting live
from the scene.

                    SCARLET
          Several buildings on the dock
          exploded, quite inexplicably. The
          fire department has put out the
          blaze and the police are
          investigating the cause of the
          fire. Miraculously, no injuries or
          deaths have been reported.

The camera's light goes off. Scarlet drops her chipper
reporter tone.

                    SCARLET
          Ugh, there is no story here. Come
          on, let's go.

Scarlet and the cameraman start for the news truck when she
notices something: ALAZANDER'S WAND.

She picks it up and examines it, then moves close enough to
whisper to the cameraman:

                    SCARLET
          We're going to the circus.

INT. BRYAN'S CAR - NIGHT

Bryan drives with Kimmy in the passenger seat.

                    BRYAN
          Just wait until I get my hands on
          that fat clown. You're going to
          see your father in action. No one
          disappoints my little girl.

EXT. CIRCUS GROUNDS - NIGHT

Bryan's car parks on the circus grounds. Bryan and Kimmy
climb out of the vehicle.

Bryan curiously looks at Pepper's trailer, riddled with
bullet holes.

INT. CIRCUS TENT - NIGHT

The tent is empty and dark. Footsteps are heard.

Bryan and Kimmy enter the seemingly empty tent.

                    BRYAN
          Hello?

No answer.

                    KIMMY
          Tubby?

Tubby emerges from the shadows.

                    TUBBY
          You two should not be here.

A smirk fills Bryan's face.

                    BRYAN
          There he is. The fat-ass who
          steals birthday cakes. I thought
          you were just a thief. Kimmy tells
          me you're into a whole lot more.

Tubby turns to Kimmy.

                    TUBBY
          You told him?

Bryan threateningly inches closer to Tubby.

                    BRYAN
          I could have have the police bring
          you in. And I will. But first, I
          have to do something. You put my
          daughter in danger and betrayed her
          trust.

POW! Bryan PUNCHES Tubby in the face. Tubby stumbles and
falls backwards. Kimmy looks torn.

                    BRYAN
          Get up, you fat bastard!

Tubby struggles to get to his feet.

Kimmy studies the tent. She notices PERFORMERS HIDING IN
THE SHADOWS.

Tubby is nearly on his feet when BRYAN HITS HIM AGAIN. He
falls back down.

                    TUBBY
          You've made your point.
               (to Kimmy)
          You have to leave. Now.

Pepper steps out of the shadows and into a bit of light.

                    KIMMY
          Pepper's back?

                    TUBBY
          Yes. We got him back. But you
          need to go. Run.

It dawns on Kimmy. Bryan laughs.

                    BRYAN
          Run? I'm not leaving until I've
          painted your entire face red with
          blood, you blimp.

                    KIMMY
          Dad, we should go.

                    BRYAN
          You wanted to watch me pummel this
          idiot. Now, you have to watch.

                    KIMMY
          No, Dad! We need to leave. NOW!

Pepper steps forward.

102.

                        PEPPER
            Mr. Mayor, if you want your
            daughter to be safe, you should
            leave now.

Bryan surveys the tent. He sees everyone in the darkness.
He sees the tiger and elephant cages lined up.

                        BRYAN
            What's going on here?

The distant sound of cars screeching, car doors opening and
closing.

Tubby grabs Kimmy's hand and pulls her toward the opposite
end of the tent. Bryan follows.

INT. CIRCUS TENT, BACKSTAGE - NIGHT

Tubby leads Kimmy and Bryan into the back room.

                        TUBBY
            Find somewhere to hide and lay low.

Tubby leaves. Bryan, confused, turns to Kimmy.

                        BRYAN
            What do you know that I don't?

                        KIMMY
            The gangsters are coming.

INT. CIRCUS TENT - NIGHT

Eerie quiet again. But this time, it is Yolanda Scarlet and
her cameraman who enter.

Tubby sighs.

                        TUBBY
                    (to himself)
            You've got to be kidding me.

Scarlet is disheartened; there is nothing going on here.

                        SCARLET
            I guess I was wrong. There is no
            story here.

Tubby emerges from the shadows.

>   TUBBY
>   We're not doing any interviews now.
>   Thanks!

The sound of more cars and doors is heard.

The camera light is switched on and Scarlet moves into
position to videotape Tubby.

>   SCARLET
>   Are you having visitors? Tell us,
>   what can we expect to happen here?

Pepper steps forward into the camera light. He smiles
broadly.

>   PEPPER
>   It's show time.

EXT. CIRCUS GROUNDS - NIGHT

A DOZEN GANGSTER CARS surround the main circus tent.
Gangsters pour out of the cars. Some form a perimeter.
Others prepare to enter the tent.

INT. CIRCUS TENT - NIGHT

Six gangsters enter the circus main stage, guns drawn.

A SPOTLIGHT SWITCHES ON! It illuminates a platform
suspended high in the air. Pepper basks in the light.

A second light - the cameraman's light - switches on.

>   PEPPER
>   Ladies and gentlemen, welcome to
>   Pepper's Groove-tastic Circus! The
>   grooviest show in the town! Prepare
>   to be astonished!

More spotlights are switched on. They're blinding. The
gangsters shield their eyes. They FIRE toward the
platform...

Acrobats swing on long ropes and kick two gangsters in the
head. The gangsters fire back wildly...

Up in the balcony, Ted grins. He flips a switch. The
lights go into strobe...

More gangsters enter, guns blazing, and fire into the
shadows...

INT. CIRCUS TENT, BACKSTAGE - NIGHT

Bryan realizes what is happening.

                    BRYAN
          There's gotta be a back way out of
          here.

He drags Kimmy to the back of the room. Through a window,
he can see more gangster cars and gangsters waiting just
outside the back exit.

                    KIMMY
          We can't go that way.

The sounds of the battle intensify.

                    KIMMY
          I need to get out there and get
          some footage for my web series.

                    BRYAN
          Absolutely not!

INT. CIRCUS TENT - NIGHT

The BATTLE ROYALE CONTINUES...

Ted shines spotlights on Zelda, who dances provocatively in
the middle of the tent. The gangsters instantly lower their
weapons, entranced by her. Their jaws hang...

Circus performers sneak up behind the gangsters and THROW
ROPES AROUND THEM...

Ted spins the spotlight to shine on a pillar platform,
illuminating Pudgey, who breaks out into a musical number...

Miss Rolly joins the action, CLUBBING PEOPLE WITH A ROLLING
PIN...

Tubby SQUIRTS WASTER at gangsters with his flower lapel...

The gangsters continue to SHOOT HAPHAZARDLY...

TIGERS ARE LET LOOSE and chase the gangsters...

                    BILLY
          Attack!

Billy WHIPS some gangsters...

IN THE BLEACHERS, Scarlet takes up a position with the melee in the background. She signals to the cameraman and begins reporting.

                    SCARLET
          As you can see, we are witnessing a
          battle between circus folk and
          gangsters.

Scarlet pulls Vlad into the shot.

                    SCARLET
          Can you tell me what the fighting
          is about?

                    VLAD
          We defend the circus against
          gangsters! You are a pretty lady.

                    SCARLET
          Why thank you!

A FIRE starts in the tent.

                    VLAD
          Things are heating up, must go!

A gangster is about to take a shot at Ted... A PIE HITS THE GANGSTER in the face, taking him down!

INT. SHERIFF BOB'S HOUSE - NIGHT

Sheriff Bob relaxes in his living room watching "Finding Bigfoot" on TV and drinking beer.

                    SHERIFF BOB
          My officers could have found this
          Big Foot by now...

RING! RING! He answers his phone.

                    SHERIFF BOB
          Yo.

On the other end is Bryan, calling from backstage.

                    BRYAN
          It's Bryan. I need you to send all
          units to the circus immediately.

                    SHERIFF BOB
          One, I quit. Two, you really need
          to get over this. It was a
          freakin' cake!

                    BRYAN
          The gangsters are attacking the
          circus. Kimmy and I are trapped in
          the main tent.

                    SHERIFF BOB
          I thought you hated the circus.

                    BRYAN
          I did! I do!
               (gathers composure)
          Look, just get on the line with the
          deputy and get everyone down here.
          Now!

                    SHERIFF BOB
          Ugh. Fine!

INT. CIRCUS TENT, BACKSTAGE - NIGHT

Bryan paces nervously.

                    BRYAN
               (calming himself)
          Sheriff Bob will bring in the
          cavalry. He'll bring officers.
          We'll be okay. He'll --

Bryan notices that Kimmy is gone.

                    BRYAN
          Kimmy? Kimmy?!

INT. CIRCUS TENT - NIGHT

Bryan pokes his head out of backstage. In the main stage,
Kimmy is crouched behind a tent pole, recording video on her
smartphone.

A gangster comes up alongside Kimmy and grabs her! Before
Bryan can react, TUBBY SMACKS THE GANGSTER ON THE HEAD WITH
A GIANT RED SHOE!

Kimmy stumbles back and falls to the ground. Tubby points
to backstage.

                    TUBBY
          Get back there!

Kimmy scoops up the smartphone and runs backstage.

Tubby and Bryan briefly make eye contact and then Tubby
rejoins the fight.

The CANNON IS FIRED and ROBERT GOES HEADFIRST INTO A GROUP
OF GANGSTERS, knocking them all down.

                    ROBERT
          Ha! Take that!

THE FIRE GROWS!

ELSEWHERE, Pepper is cornered by Frankie Slapnuts.

                    FRANK SLAPNUTS
          If you had just signed the
          document...

IN THE BLEACHERS, Miss Scarlet watches. Her cameraman
records the action. THEN, A FLASH OF SMOKE AND LIGHT! A
visibly wounded Alazander appears next to Scarlet.

                    ALAZANDER
          I believe you have something of
          mine.

She smiles and hands him the wand.

                    ALAZANDER
          I appreciate it, very much.

Alazander points the wand and FIRES MAGIC at Frankie
Slapnuts. FRANKIE'S PANTS ARE ON FIRE! He prances around
then rolls on the ground to put the fire out.

PEPPER STOMPS FRANKIE IN THE GROIN.

INT. CIRCUS TENT, BACKSTAGE - NIGHT

Bryan smells the fire.

                    BRYAN
          Fire! Kimmy, we can't stay back
          here. We need to make a run for
          it.

                    KIMM
          Through the main stage?

                    BRYAN
          The backdoor. There are some
          gangsters out there, but if we're
          fast - real fast - we'll be okay.
          Can you be fast?

108.

                    KIMMY
          Yes.

Bryan leads Kimmy to the back stage exit. They are about to
step through, but are pushed back by someone entering: BIG
LOU.

                    BIG LOU
          Well, well, if it isn't the new
          mayor who hates me so much!

Bryan says nothing.

                    BIG LOU
          I came here just to talk reason
          with the Ringmaster. To get him to
          sell this dump. But to find you
          here, in the middle of this
          battle... Looks as though
          Christmas came early this year!

Bryan grabs Kimmy's hand and they run into the main stage.

INT. CIRCUS TENT - NIGHT

Bryan and Kimmy find themselves in the middle of the battle,
surrounded by dueling gangsters and circus folk. FIRE and
SMOKE fill the tent. It is NIGHTMARISH.

Big Lou approaches Bryan. Bryan shields Kimmy with his
body. Big Lou raises a pistol.

                    BIG LOU
          Goodbye, Mr. Mayor.

TUBBY STEPS BETWEEN THEM.

                    TUBBY
          I don't think so.

BANG!

SLOW-MOTION: The bullet bounces off of Tubby's blubber and
ricochets away!

Unaffected, Tubby stares at Big Lou.

Horror fills Big Lou's eyes.

                    BIG LOU
          No. No one is _that_ fat!

TUBBY CHARGES AT BIG LOU! The two wrestle!

Two gangsters rush over, but A PIECE OF FIERY DEBRIS FALLS between Tubby and Big Lou and the gangsters -- they're cut off!

Tubby gets to his feet. Big Lou looks for the pistol -- it's trapped under burning wood.

The SMOKE IS BLINDING. Big Lou has trouble seeing.

Tubby calls up to Pudgey.

                    TUBBY
          NOW!

Pudgey is up on a high-wire, riding the unicycle. She balances it, draws a knife, and cuts a rope.

A TIGER CAGE falls from above and traps Big Lou.

POLICE SIRENS BLARE FROM OUTSIDE.

                    FRANK SLAPNUTS
          Police!

Frankie, cupping his groin, leads the gangsters out of the tent. Big Lou remains stuck in the tiger cage. Tubby stands guard over the cage.

Sheriff Bob and a dozen officers enter the tent.

Bryan and Kimmy approach the cage. Bryan and Tubby make eye contact -- a silent thank you.

Sheriff Bob approaches.

                    BRYAN
          Cuff him! Then get the hell out of
          here!

MORE FIERY DEBRIS FALLS from above.

                    SHERIFF BOB
          Big Lou, you're under arrest.

Tubby opens the tiger cage. Sheriff Bob places cuffs on Big Lou.

EXT. CIRCUS GROUNDS - NIGHT

The burning tent illuminates the circus grounds.

Tubby, Bryan, Kimmy, Sheriff Bob and Big Lou run out of the
tent. Tubby rushes over to where Pepper and Pudgey are
waiting and embraces them.

Police officers arrest many of gangsters. Big Lou is placed
inside a police car.

                    BRYAN
          Good! Round up all the gangsters!

Kimmy gazes worriedly at Tubby. Bryan notices this and
kneels down beside her.

                    BRYAN
          He was working for them.

Kimmy turns to Sheriff Bob, tears forming in his eyes.

                    KIMMY
          Tubby was undercover. To help
          catch the gangsters and get the
          reward. Right?

                    SHERIFF BOB
          Oh yeah. Right.

Bryan turns to Sheriff Bob with an angry look.

                    KIMMY
          Then Tubby is off the hook. Right,
          dad?

Bryan considers this for a moment. Tears form in Kimmy's
eyes.

Bryan smiles and puts an arm around her.

                    BRYAN
          Right.

Kimmy embraces her father. The relationship is repaired.

Scarlet rushes over to Pepper.

                    SCARLET
          Your circus has been destroyed.
          What is going through your head
          right now?

                    PEPPER
          Did you get it all on camera?

                    SCARLET
          Why, yes.

                    PEPPER
          Good. Because this was the show of
          a lifetime!

The circus folk CHEER!

Pudgey and Tubby kiss.

                    KIMMY
          Gross.

CHEERS continue! The circus folk embrace one another. Fire
engines arrive to put out the blaze.

Kimmy approaches Miss Scarlet.

                    KIMMY
          Excuse me, Miss Scarlet?

                    SCARLET
          Yes?

                    KIMMY
          Can I have a copy of your footage?

                    SCARLET
          Whatever for?

                    KIMMY
          My web series. Chasing Tubby,
          episode 2.

Scarlet smiles.

                    SCARLET
          Of course!

INT. MAYOR'S OFFICE - DAY

Tubby, Alazander, and Pepper sit across from Bryan. Kimmy
stands behind her father, smiling broadly. Sheriff Bob
stands off to the side.

Bryan reluctantly hands Tubby a check.

                    BRYAN
          The reward, for the capture of Big
          Lou.

                    TUBBY
          Thank you.

They all rise.

                    BRYAN
          Maybe you can buy your own cake
          from now on.

                    TUBBY
          No. This money is to rebuild.

Tubby hands the check out to Pepper.

                    PEPPER
          I don't want the money.

                    TUBBY
          You'll need it to re-open the
          circus.

                    PEPPER
          I am not re-opening the circus.

Bryan can't help to visually express his joy.

                    TUBBY
          What?!

                    PEPPER
          I'm giving the circus to you and
          Alazander. Boys, it's yours now.

Bryan lowers his head onto his desk in disappointment.

                    TUBBY
          You're quitting now? We're on a
          roll!
               (beat)
          I could go for some eggs and bacon
          on a roll...

Pepper places her arms on Tubby's shoulders.

                    PEPPER
          Tubby, that last performance was
          the one I waited for my entire
          life! I've accomplished my goal.
          I'm retiring.

                    ALAZANDER
          Ringmaster, this is an honor. Thank
          you.

                    PEPPER
          I know you'll do fantastic, groovy
          things with the circus. If you two
          can get along.

                    ALAZANDER
          If we must.

Pepper smiles broadly. Pepper, Tubby, and Alazander exit.

                    BRYAN
          Well, now that the sappiness is
          over, let's get back to work.
                    (to Sheriff Bob)
          Have you located Mr. Mudword?

                    SHERIFF BOB
          He is nowhere to be found.

                    BRYAN
          Keep looking.

Sheriff Bob smiles.

                    SHERIFF BOB
          With pleasure.

INT. CITY HALL, HALLWAY - DAY

Tubby stops Alazander and Pepper.

                    TUBBY
          Look, I am going to need to skim
          some money off the top of that. I
          need to make things right.

INT. LAUNDROMAT - DAY (MONTAGE)

A mailman hands the old lady an envelop. She opens it to
find a WAD OF CASH.

INT. BIKE SHOP - DAY (MONTAGE)

The bike store owner and some employees stare at another WAD
OF CASH on the counter.

114.

INT. RESTAURANT - DAY (MONTAGE)

The restaurant owner opens a check holder. Inside, there is
a NOTE and an LARGE TIP. The note reads: "I'm sorry."

INT. NEWLYWED'S HOUSE - DAY (MONTAGE)

The Bride is flipping through their wedding album, which
consists entirely of PHOTOS OF CAKE.

The Groom sits down beside her, holding a box. He opens it.
Inside is the TOP OF A WEDDING CAKE and a note.

He opens the note: "I saved you the top! Congrats!"

INT. KIMMY'S HOUSE, LIVING ROOM - DAY (MONTAGE)

A delivery man hands Bryan a package. Bryan sets it down on
the dining room table and opens it.

Inside is a CAKE. Written in icing on top: "Here's your
cake back."

INT. ROLAND'S HOUSE - DAY (MONTAGE)

KNOCK! KNOCK!

Roland, the hardware store owner, opens the front door to
reveal Tubby.

Tubby holds out an envelop.

                    TUBBY
          I hope this is enough to rebuild
          your hardware store.

The old man takes it. He peaks inside the envelop. His
eyes light up. He gazes at Tubby. He is confused.

                    TUBBY (CONT'D)
          I'm going to need your help to
          rebuild the circus. It's in pretty
          bad shape.

EXT. CIRCUS GROUNDS - DAY

The main tent is a pile of smoldering rubble. Tubby,
Pudgey, and Kimmy gaze at it.

At their feet, a battered and burned sign reads "Pepper's
Groove-tastic Circus."

                    KIMMY
          As your new marketing director, I
          suggest we change the name of the
          circus.

                    TUBBY
          Fine. But that's all that's
          changing! Now, run along and come
          up with some new names.

Kimmy leaves.

Pudgey leans her head against Tubby's fat shoulder.

                    PUDGEY
          Rebuilding is going to be a lot of
          work.

                    TUBBY
          Yup.

                    PUDGEY
          It's going to take a lot of time.

                    TUBBY
          Yup.

                    PUDGEY
          What will you do in the meantime?

Tubby smiles broadly.

                    TUBBY
          I could go for some cake.

INT. FUN CENTER - DAY

Ginger's birthday party. THE BIRTHDAY CAKE sits on a table
just in front of the batting cages.

All the children, including Kimmy and Jacob, gather around.

ON THE OTHER END OF THE ROOM, Tubby peeks around the corner.
He licks his lips.

Tubby's about to make a move for it...

Then, a GIANT RAT APPEARS OUT OF NOWHERE, SCOOPS UP THE
CAKE, and runs!

                    TUBBY
          Hey, that's my cake!

Tubby runs after the Giant Rat.

EXT. SUBURBAN STREETS - DAY

Tubby chases the Giant Rat down the block, but he cannot
keep pace with him.

The Giant Rat turns a corner and disappears.

Tubby stops to catch his breath. Defeated.

Kimmy runs up alongside Tubby.

                    KIMMY
          Uh-oh. Looks like you've got
          competition.

                                        FADE TO BLACK.

TITLE CARD: "TUBBY WILL BE BACK..."

THE END.